HOME
IN A WILDERNESS FORT

COPPER HARBOR, 1844

Home in a Wilderness Fort: Copper Harbor 1844
Copyright ©2006 Charlotte Otten

ISBN 13   978-0-9766104-5-8
ISBN 10   0-9766104-5-0

Printed in the United States of America

Arbutus Press
Traverse City, Michigan
editor@arbutuspress.com
www.Arbutuspress.com

Library of Congress Cataloging-in-Publication Data

Otten, Charlotte F.
 Home in a wilderness fort: Copper Harbor, 1844/ Charlotte Otten.
        p. cm.
 Summary: After moving up to Copper Harbor on Michigan's Upper Peninsula to live in Fort Wilkins in 1844, ten-year-old Josette proceeds to make friends with everyone she meets especially Maria, an Ojibwa Indian, who teaches her many new skills to help her adjust to her new home.
 Includes bibliographic references.
 ISBN 0-9766104-5-0
 [1. Orphans—Fiction. 2. Sisters—Fiction. 3. Friendship—Fiction. 4. Ojibwa Indians—Fiction. 5. Indians of North America—Fiction. 6. Frontier and pioneer life—Michigan—Copper Harbor—Fiction. 7. Fort Wilkins (Mich.)—History—19th century—Fiction] I. Title.

PZ7.O8783Ho 2006
[Fic}—dc22

                              2005037869

Cover illustration: Lori Wheldon

DEDICATION

To Stephanie and Chelsea

HOME
IN A WILDERNESS FORT

COPPER HARBOR, 1844

Charlotte Otten

Arbutus Press
Traverse City, Michigan

CHAPTER ONE

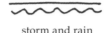

storm and rain

"Careful, little lady," the sailor shouted as he reached out a big hand to keep Josette from sliding off the slippery deck. Josette was happy to be breathing fresh air. This was her sixteenth day on board the *John Jacob Astor*. They had set sail on Lake Superior from Sault Ste. Marie, Michigan, and for fifteen days she had been seasick and confined to her cabin. To keep passengers from throwing up, the sailors had delivered dry crackers to the cabins, and while storms pushed the *John Jacob Astor* around like a toy boat in the middle of an ocean, passengers spent the time trying not to roll out of their bunks.

Night and day the ship battled pounding waves. Waves twenty feet high rolled over the deck, almost sinking the vessel. Icy cold water seeped into the cabins and covered the floor ankle-deep. For fifteen days the wind did not stop howling. It made such eerie, high-pitched sounds that Josette's ears ached. Every time they struck a deep trough, her stomach heaved—up and down, up and down—to the rhythms of the waves.

Sometimes the ship lurched and was quiet for a moment, almost standing still at the top of a big wave before it trembled and plunged, waiting for the next big wave to take it back up over the top. Everyone was afraid that every next wave would toss them all into the cold waters of Lake Superior.

By the twelfth day, the passengers had almost lost hope of reaching Copper Harbor alive. They thought they would drown, still seasick, in water that still held chunks of winter ice.

Josette was the only child on board. Until late June of 1844, she had never left Fredericksburg, Virginia, where she had lived with her sister and her brother-in-law since the death of her parents. When her mother and father had died of typhoid fever within a week of each other, her sister, Edith, and husband, Edmund Elliott, took Josette in immediately and made her feel that she belonged to them.

A few weeks after her tenth birthday, when Josette was just beginning to get over the death of her parents, her brother-in-law, Edmund, has just walked into their kitchen where Josette and Edith were eating breakfast. Josette jumped up and hugged him. "Oh Edmund," she said, "you're back. I was lonely without you.

Edmund walked over to the table and hugged and kissed Edith. He said, "It looks like we'll be leaving Virginia for a while. My regiment is being called up to go set up a fort in Copper Harbor, Michigan."

"How far away from Fredericksburg is Michigan?" his young wife asked.

Edmund didn't want to worry her. "It's quite a long ride," he said, "but we'll travel first by railroad to Detroit and then by ship to Copper Harbor." Edmund was a 1st Lieutenant in Company A under Captain Clary, who commanded the 105 men of Companies A and B.

"May I go along, too? " Josette asked. She was

afraid they would leave her behind and there would be no one who would take her in. She didn't care how far away Michigan was as long as she could stay with Edith and Edmund.

"Of course," Edmund said. "We'd never leave you behind. You're part of our family."

"What would we do without you," added Edith, "especially since I'm having a baby in September?"

Before Edith could ask her husband whether there were doctors or midwives in northern Michigan to help in the delivery of her baby, Edmund said, "We'll have to be ready to leave by the first of next week."

"Will I be able to take my piano?" Edith asked.

"Yes," said Edmund. "My Captain promised there would be room for your piano. He said they could use some music up there in the North, especially for Christmas." Edmund knew that Edith couldn't live without her piano. She played every day and often sang when she played. She had taught Josette to play, too, and the two sisters liked to play together and sing duets.

By the first of the week they had packed a trunk and boarded the train to Detroit. Edith found it hard to leave her friends, but Josette was eager for adventure. She couldn't wait to see Copper Harbor. She wondered why it was called Copper Harbor, and she had many other questions. "Will there be Indians up there?" she asked Edmund. He said he hoped not.

By the first of the week, they had sent their furniture ahead to Copper Harbor. With a large trunk, they boarded the train for Detroit, then sailed along the eastern shore of Lake Huron. When they got to the "Soo" they waited to get across to Lake Superior. Josette fell asleep. She was tired from all the sleepless days and nights of their trip.

The next thing she knew, Edmund was lifting her down on a dock and pointing to the ship that would take them to Copper Harbor and they finally boarded the ship, the *John Jacob Astor*.

What a long trip! Josette wondered sometimes if they would ever reach Copper Harbor and Fort Wilkins.

Now their sixteenth day on the water, they were told they would land in Copper Harbor, a place one of the sailors described as "the end of the world." The sailor who had grabbed Josette's hand to keep her safe smiled at the young girl. "That's quite a storm we've had," he said, "but you still have to be careful on deck, even if the storm is over. It's very slippery from fifteen days of waves washing over it."

"Will we get to Copper Harbor today?" Josette asked.

"Why don't you go down and get some breakfast," said the sailor, "and by the time you get back up here, we'll be able to see Copper Harbor."

For the first time since Sault Ste. Marie, Josette felt hungry at the mention of food.

"They have some delicious flapjacks," the sailor said, "and be sure that they give you a slice of ham, too."

"Before I get breakfast," Josette said, "can you tell me about Indians?"

"I'll tell you right now," said the sailor. "I've never seen an Indian at Copper Harbor, but I know they're there. They're there, and they're dangerous. They make white people disappear."

"How do you know Indians are dangerous if you've never seen one?" asked Josette curiously. "Have you ever seen anyone disappear?"

The sailor laughed. "I guess you have me there,"

he said, "but you'd better be careful when you get to Copper Harbor. Why do you think your brother-in-law was sent up here?"

"I don't know," said Josette. "He said that he was going to help build Fort Wilkins."

"And what do you think Fort Wilkins is for?" asked the sailor.

"I don't know," replied Josette frankly.

"To guard against Indians. The miners are afraid of them. The Indians signed a treaty with the United States government in 1843 and were paid good money for the land, and the government set up reservations where Indians could stay. Then the government encouraged miners to stake out land so they could explore it for copper. There were stories that copper gleamed in rivers and lakes, sometimes with copper rocks so big no one could lift them. The Indians agreed not to bother the miners and to allow mining companies to establish claims. But you listen to me, little lady," he said. "Indians are still hanging around. Some of them are still living on Isle Royale and a few are living in L'Anse, but plenty of them are still around Copper Harbor, and they're sneaky. They hide behind trees, they shoot arrows and kill animals, they have war dances, and they come up behind you and scalp you."

Josette didn't want to believe him. What Indian would want the scalp of a ten-year-old girl? "Have you ever seen an Indian scalp anyone?" she asked.

The sailor laughed. "You don't believe anything I've said, do you?" he said. "Well, you listen to me, little lady. When I come back this way a couple of years from now, I want to make sure there'll be a little girl named Josette still alive."

"By that time I'll be a big girl," Josette corrected him with a smile.

The sailor pointed across the deck. "Ask that man about Indians. He's the owner of a copper mine."

The man walking toward them smiled at Josette.

"Have you ever seen an Indian?" she asked him.

"Not in Copper Harbor," the man answered, "but I've seen them trading furs and fishing in long canoes. They haven't bothered me or my miners, but we're glad that soldiers have come up here to protect us from them."

"What will the soldiers have to do?" she asked. She couldn't picture Edmund shooting a gun at Indians.

"They'll keep an eye out for Indians and warn them not to mess with us." Suddenly the man remembered something. "When I was digging in the mine," he said, "I found a birchbark scroll."

"What did it say?" asked Josette.

"Indians don't write in English, and I can't read their pictures. The scroll is all pictures."

"Do you have the scroll with you?" asked Josette.

"No, but if you come to my cabin in Copper Harbor I'll be glad to show it to you."

"How will I find you?"

"Here's my name," he said, writing it on a slip of paper. "Just ask anyone in Copper Harbor, and they'll point you to my cabin."

"I'll come," said Josette. "Maybe we can figure out the pictures on the scroll together." She suddenly changed the subject. "Do you have any daughters my age?" She was beginning to think how strange it would feel to be the only girl at Fort Wilkins or in Copper Harbor.

"No," the man answered. "I hope you won't be lonely at Fort Wilkins."

Just then Edith and Edmund came up on the deck. "We were looking for you, Josette," Edith said.

"I was talking to my new friends about Indians," she told them.

"We can talk about Indians in the days ahead," said Edmund. "This morning, how about breakfast?"

"The sailor told me they have flapjacks and ham."

"Ham!" sighed Edith. "That reminds me of our home in Virginia. I can still smell hams curing in the smokehouse."

"Have a good breakfast," said the sailor, adding to Josette, "and you'll be able to see Copper Harbor in the distance after you're finished. We're getting close."

As the family went below again in search of breakfast, the sailor thought about the harbor they would be entering shortly. He knew how treacherous it was, filled with rocks hiding just below the surface. Were those hidden rocks filled with copper as rumor had it? Copper or not, they were dangerous. And there were shoals, shallow, rocky reefs that trapped ships in suddenly shallow water. Many ships had broken up on those rocks. Even experienced sailors in fur traders' canoes had run aground on the shoals.

The harbor entrance was between a large rock at the end of a reef that ran east from Porter's Island and the point of land on the east side of the entrance. The course was south until within 250 yards of the rock, then west one and one-quarter miles to the anchorage at the head of the bay. Once at the anchorage they would be safe.

He hoped there wouldn't be a sudden gale. The sky over Lake Superior could be blue one minute and dark as night the next, and if there were a heavy wind, it would be hard to enter the harbor without being blown off course. Then their ship would be dashed on the rocks. And there would be no one to rescue them.

The sailor decided to keep on eye on little Josette if anything should happen to the ship. He couldn't bear to think of her drowning.

CHAPTER TWO

fort

After breakfast, back on the deck watching for Copper Harbor to appear on the coastline, Josette felt better than she had in two whole weeks. "Look," she said to the sailor, "everything's green!"

"It's a relief after gray water and gray sky," said the sailor.

"Look at the green hills and mountains," Josette said to her sister, who was also on the deck waiting to see the harbor and set foot on dry land.

"This is different from the Blue Ridge Mountains of Virginia," commented Edith.

"That's because the trees up here are mostly white pines, white cedars, maples, oaks, and birches," said the sailor. "They're not blue like Virginia spruce trees."

"Is that all that's up here?" Edith asked. "Only trees?"

"That's about right," said the sailor, "along with a few miners and soldiers."

"There's an eagle," said Josette suddenly, pointing to a large bird in flight. It was flying over a mountain that towered over the hills, about 700 feet high. The sun shone on the eagle's wings.

"What's that big box in the tree at the top of mountain?" Josette asked the sailor.

"That's the eagle's nest," he replied. "Ever since I've been sailing up here, I've watched that nest grow bigger, and I've seen the same eagle flying above it, probably protecting the young eaglets in the nest."

A rumble in the distance sounded like thunder. The sailor knew the ship was still in dangerous waters, and he looked at the sky, but there was no sign of an approaching storm. The sky was cloudless.

"Was that thunder?" Edith asked.

"No ma'am," said the sailor. "That's the sound of miners blasting solid rock in the mines. You'll hear that all day when you're up at the fort."

As the ship got closer to the harbor, the sailor said to Josette, "We're going to have a good landing."

Josette was breathless as the Captain steered the ship skillfully past Porter's Island and eased between the rocks. As they sailed into the sheltered harbor, safe from storms and rocks and shoals, everyone on deck applauded.

"What's that shining in the water?" Josette asked.

"That's a lump of copper," said her new friend. "If you go wading in the brook that runs not far from the grounds of the fort, you might see copper glistening in the rocks."

"Will I get rich if I save it?" Josette asked.

"You'll have to talk to the miners about that," he said, "but I doubt it. It takes tons of copper before it turns it into money."

Suddenly seagulls surrounded the ship, crying a welcome to everyone on board, and one of them landed on the railing close to Josette. It was a young gull that still had brown feathers. Even its beak was still brown, not like the other gulls with their bright yellow beaks with a bright red dot on the end. Josette found a cracker in her pocket, left over from when she had been seasick, and held out a piece of it to the young gull. He grabbed it, flew away, then quickly came back. This time a flock of gulls followed him and perched on the rail, watching the young gull and waiting for crackers from Josette. She broke off another piece of cracker and the young one took it from her hand. "Can I take this gull to the fort with me for a pet?" she asked Edith and Edmund.

"Gulls like their freedom," said Edmund, who had his hand on Josette's shoulder to make sure she didn't slip off the deck if they hit a rock, "but this one's still young. He's taken a liking to you. Maybe he'll find you at the fort."

"I wouldn't count on it," said the sailor. "What I'd count on is bears. You be sure to watch out for them."

The ship slowed as it drew nearer and nearer to the shore. Then gradually they were landing at a dock, and above their heads, riding high over the beautiful blue waters of Lake Superior, was the flag of the United States. Everyone saluted the flag and cheered.

Now Josette could see the buildings of Copper Harbor huddled along the shore. There were only a few rough-hewn pine buildings, but there were many tents. "That's where the miners live," the sailor told her.

"The buildings don't look at all like the houses in Fredericksburg," said Edith.

"Wait 'til you see the houses at the fort," the sailor said to Edith. "They're clapboard painted white. The officers' houses are really nice, with big fireplaces and verandas stretching across the front."

Edith smiled. "We'll need a comfortable house when this baby comes," she said.

As she got off the ship, Josette swayed back and forth, trying to find her balance. She was so used to the rocking ship that she had forgotten how to walk on solid ground that didn't lurch like turbulent waves. She lifted her right leg up ridiculously high, and then her left leg flew up high. Edith and Edmund laughed, but their feet also flew up and down and sidewise. It took a while before their feet became comfortable walking on land.

Two soldiers from the Fort were waiting for Edmund. "Reporting to Lieutenant Elliott, Private Wilks and Private Hawkins!" They saluted, and Edmund returned the salute and introduced Edith and Josette. Then the other soldiers on the *John Jacob Astor*, who were also assigned to Fort Wilkins, joined the group. Privates Wilks and Hawkins had brought horses and wagons for transporting the trunks and supplies for the fort. "I'll take all the trunks back to the fort," said Private Wilks, "and then I'll come back for you, sir. While you're waiting, you can get good food at the *Astor*."

Private Hawkins said, "I've got a number of items to unload and take back to the fort, one of them very heavy. Two soldiers can help me, and the rest can eat at the *Astor* with you. I'll see you at the fort."

"Where's the *Astor*?" Edmund asked, taking charge of the soldiers as their commanding officer.

"Over there." Private Wilks pointed to a pine log structure, one and one-half stories high and twenty-four feet long by sixteen feet wide.

François, who was cook, waiter, porter, clerk and "chambermaid," greeted them at the *Astor* and led them to a long table made of two boards laid upon sawhorses.

"Come, come, sit down. I have good food for you." He disappeared briefly, quickly returning with steaming bowls of food. Josette tried to guess what was in them. François explained, "This bowl, venison in gravy. This one, roast porcupine, tastes like young pig. This one, whitefish in butter. This one, roast pigeons. This one, potatoes. But first, you have corn and bean soup. After, shortcake for everybody, with rum for the soldiers, cream for the lady and the little girl."

He bowed, and Josette felt as though she were eating in a fine hotel in Fredericksburg. After trying all the dishes, Edith said the food was delicious. She liked the roast pigeons best.

Before they left, Josette asked François about Indians. "Do you ever see them? Do they come to Copper Harbor?"

François shrugged. "Sometime I think I hear them at night. But maybe no. Maybe bear. They do not come to the *Astor*."

By the time they had finished their sumptuous meal, the wagon was standing outside waiting to give them a ride to the fort.

"Come again," François said to Josette. "I get lonely. Only miners and soldiers here. My family in France. I have little girl like you. Next year I go back. She be big by that time."

Josette promised to come see him again after they were settled at the fort.

"Where's my piano?" Edith asked Private Wilks. She suddenly remembered that the piano had sailed with them.

"It's on its way to the fort," said Private Wilks. "The other wagon took it. That's the heavy item he was talking about. I'm sure it's in your house by now."

"I couldn't live here without my piano," said Edith.

While Josette and Edith rode in the wagon, Edmund and the soldiers walked behind them. There was no road to the fort, only a rough wagon track. The trees were so close, Edith and the driver had to duck so as not to get caught in low-hanging branches. The woods smelled of pungent pinesap.

Josette noticed a gun lying behind her in the wagon. "What's that gun for?" she asked the soldier.

"That's just in case we see an Indian," he said.

"Do you shoot Indians?" she asked.

"I've never even seen one. But that's why we're here. In case the Indians give the miners trouble."

"I'd like to see an Indian," she said.

"You won't see one if you stay close to the fort. Sometimes I have a strange feeling that Indians come to the fort at night when we're sleeping, even though soldiers stand guard all night. Indians are so quiet you'll never know if one is behind a tree, or behind your house. So be careful," he said.

The track turned and twisted. The soldiers had cut down just enough trees to get a wagon to and from the fort. Even though they could hear Lake Superior slapping against the rocks, they couldn't see the water because their way was completely enclosed by trees.

After about a mile, they reached a clearing, and there stood the beginnings of the fort. The first thing Josette saw was the flag of the United States waving in a gentle breeze. Then she saw that the fort was arranged in a U-shape. A long lake, not Lake Superior but some smaller body of water, reflected the trees that surrounded it.

"I wonder which house is ours," Josette said to Edith.

"The officers' houses are finished," said Private Wilks, "and we're building the quarters for the enlisted men. Some civilians are helping us so the fort will be finished before winter comes. Those tents over there are for us soldiers while the quarters are being finished."

"Is it cold in the tents?" Josette asked him.

"We've got heavy blankets," he said. "I'll drop you off in front of your house."

Private Wilks helped Edith down from the wagon as Josette jumped quickly and eagerly to the ground.

Edmund appeared from around the bend in the road, followed by his men, and said, "Well, let's see our house."

Edith couldn't believe how nice it was. It had a parlor where the soldiers had already put Edith's piano, and an adjoining dining room. In one corner was a big woodstove to keep them warm in winter. There was a kitchen with both an open fireplace and a cookstove. The house had three bedrooms upstairs, and one was just for Josette. It had a window looking out on the lake.

"Oh look," said Edith, "our furniture is all set out for us with tables and chairs and beds and cooking utensils." There was even a neat stack of wood for them to burn right away in case they wanted to cook a home meal their first night in the house, although no one thought of being hungry after their big dinner at the *Astor*. Edith did not mention Fredericksburg or compare this house to their Virginia home.

Josette suddenly remembered something. "I forgot to say 'Goodbye' to the sailor. I don't even know his name. Do you think I'll ever see him again?"

"I'll get the schedule of the ships coming into Copper Harbor, and maybe he'll be on one of them," said Edmund. "Then I'll make sure that you see him again. Right now I'm going to report to Captain Clary, and after that, I'll get us some supplies. I'll be gone for a while."

"I'll start unpacking the trunk," said Edith.

"I'm going to look at the lake," said Josette.

"Be careful," said Edith. "Don't fall in."

As Edmund and Josette were leaving the house, they could hear Edith at the piano playing "Now Thank We All Our God." Even though the piano was a little out of tune, the music sounded wonderful to Edmund. As he and Josette walked toward the Captain's quarters, he hummed the song, thankful that Edith seemed so happy up here in the North, hundreds of miles from her home in Virginia, at the northernmost post in the United States, way at the tip of the Keweenaw Peninsula.

Josette and Edmund stopped on the shore of the lake.

"This lake looks small," said Josette. "I can see the trees on the other side."

"It is small in comparison with Lake Superior," said Edmund, "but it's big enough. It looks deep."

They walked a little farther. "Here are two canoes!" Josette exclaimed in surprise.

"I suppose the soldiers use them to go fishing," said Edmund absent-mindedly. "I'm going to the Captain's quarters now, and I'll be gone for most of the afternoon." He paused, and then looked into the little girl's eyes. "Be careful, Josette. We don't want to lose you."

Josette wondered why everyone was always telling her to be careful.

CHAPTER THREE

canoe

After standing on the shore of the lake for a while and watching minnows swimming in pools of light near the shore, Josette thought it might be nice to sit in one of the canoes and pretend she was paddling on the clear, blue water. She was sure it would be safe because the ripples on the water were not like the big waves on Lake Superior. These ripples couldn't carry her far away.

Before getting into the canoe, she took off her bonnet. She wanted to feel warm sunshine on her face and a gentle breeze fluttering through her long hair after so many days of gray skies and heavy rain on board ship. She laid her bonnet in the other canoe so that it wouldn't get grass stains or mud on it, stepped into "her" canoe and edged her way to the far end to get a better look at the lake.

It was longer than she had thought. She couldn't see the end in either direction. She stroked the paddle and pretended to leave the shore. Then she took the paddle and dug it into the pebbly shore, pushing gently. The canoe began to move slowly. Then, to her surprise, the wind gusted and pushed the canoe away from shore—not very far from shore, just a little.

Josette tried to push her way back to shore by digging the paddle into the lake bottom, but instead of pushing the canoe backward, she pushed it forward, where the wind caught it and carried it farther out into the lake. She saw that the lake was gradually getting deeper. Minnows disappeared. A large fish swam close to the canoe. She couldn't touch bottom with the paddle. She had never seen anyone paddle a canoe, so she didn't know how to get back to shore.

Josette wasn't worried. She thought the wind that pushed her out into the lake would push her back to shore somewhere not far from the Fort. Instead, the wind kept pushing the canoe farther from the shore.

The canoe turned slowly a couple of times, then drifted to the middle of the lake. It moved gently at first, not fast enough to make Josette feel afraid. Then it picked up a little speed. She could still see her house, but from the middle of the lake it looked far away.

She called, "Edith, Edith . . ." but Edith was busy indoors with her unpacking and didn't hear Josette call.

The canoe drifted past the house and past all the cleared land of the fort. Now all Josette could see was tall grass and even taller trees. She was leaving the fort behind, and she didn't know where she was going. She couldn't see the end of the lake.

As she drifted away from the fort and from her house, she wondered where she would land. Would there be bears or Indians on the shore? She thought she saw bushes moving slightly on one side of the shore. Could there be Indians in the bushes waiting to capture her? Something black shook the bushes. A mother bear and her two cubs pushed through the grasses and trees.

They came to the shore of the lake. The mother bear looked at Josette in the canoe, but the bear didn't make a sound. Josette didn't make a sound, either. Josette hoped the mother bear couldn't swim.

The cubs paid no attention to Josette. Suddenly the mother bear started wading in the water, heading toward the canoe. She was big enough to tip the canoe over! Just as suddenly she stopped, looked at Josette, and then she dipped her paw into the water and scooped up a fish. She carried it in her mouth back into the woods. The cubs followed her. They were going to have a raw fish dinner somewhere in the forest.

Josette had seen her first bears, and they hadn't attacked her.

She kept on drifting in the canoe, farther and farther away from the fort. Now she was getting worried, but she remembered that there was still the other canoe onshore back by the house. As soon as Edith and Edmund knew that one canoe was missing, they would suppose that she was in the other, somewhere on the lake. They would ask a couple of soldiers at the fort to get into the other canoe and look for Josette. The lake had to end somewhere. The soldiers would be sure to find her. The soldiers knew where the lake ended.

Gradually the canoe began to slow down, but then it suddenly speeded up again, twisting and turning, almost tipping her out, and finally making a big turn out of the lake into a fast-flowing stream. Cliffs on both sides of the stream seemed to be closing in on her as the canoe sped along, faster and faster. Before she knew what was happening, she was being swept over a waterfall! She couldn't escape from the canoe unless she plunged right out into the waterfall!

Where was she going? The canoe moved faster and

faster, then jerked to a stop, pitching Josette forward, off balance. She was afraid she might hit her head on a big rock at the bottom of the waterfall. The bottom of the canoe scraped on gravel and small rocks. Then the water stopped rushing, and Josette could see the bottom of the stream at last.

She hopped out of the canoe, looked around and saw that the stream flowed into a very big lake. She dragged the canoe onto the shore of the big lake. She didn't want to let it drift away, even if she wasn't in it. Could this be Lake Superior? It looked a lot like that lake she had sailed on for sixteen days. If it were, Copper Harbor must be close by, she thought. But which way?

She couldn't decide whether to try walking along the rocky shore of Lake Superior to try to find Copper Harbor where François could help her, or to take off her shoes and wade in the stream and lake back to the fort. The problem with wading back was that the waterfall and the grass and trees were so high that she knew she wouldn't be able to see where she was going. She didn't want to get lost in the woods on her way back.

Before making up her mind what to do, whether to walk along the shore of Lake Superior to Copper Harbor or to wade in the stream and in the smaller lake, she sat down to think over the alternatives.

Maybe it would be best just to stay here with the canoe until Edmund and his men came looking for her in the other canoe. That might be a long time because they wouldn't know which way she had drifted, so maybe it would be night before they found her. What if they didn't find her before dark? It would be cold on the shore. Besides, night was the time that Indians came out of hiding. What if Indians found her and took her back with them? Then no one would ever find her. She might never see Edith and Edmund again.

I'll try to walk along Lake Superior first, she thought to herself. I know François will help me in Copper Harbor. She looked up to see in what direction the sun was moving. She thought Copper Harbor was where the sun was shining.

Josette left the cove and the canoe and started walking along the shore of Lake Superior. At first it wasn't hard to walk on the small rocks and pebbles along the shore. She stopped to look at stones that gleamed in the sunlight, picking up those that had copper streaks in them. Some of the stones looked like they were solid copper, they were so shiny. She put the shiniest stones in her pockets. She would show them to Edith and Edmund when she got back, as well as to the miner she had met on the ship.

Soon the shore changed from small rocks and pebbles to larger rocks. Ahead of her was a huge boulder, and beyond that boulder, as far as she could see, there were even bigger boulders. How would she ever get past them? Could she climb over them? What if she fell or sprained an ankle or broke a leg? Then nobody would ever find her. They might think she had been carried off by Indians and had disappeared.

Maybe she could wade out into Lake Superior past the huge boulders, but what if the lake was so deep that she drowned?

Josette turned around and started walking back to the canoe, which she could still see in the distance. As she walked, she picked up more copper stones. I can save them in the canoe, she thought. When she reached the canoe, she put down her copper stones and sat down next to them. The canoe felt safe. It wasn't moving.

After a rest, she decided to try wading back to the fort by way of the stream and lake. She took off her shoes and stockings and put them in the canoe next to the shining stones. Since there was no shore along the stream, she waded along the edge. First the water covered her ankles, and then it came halfway up her legs. It was cold, and the stream's bottom was covered with rocks that hurt Josette's feet. She bumped her big toe on a hidden rock. Ouch! She could hardly wiggle it. She hoped it wasn't broken.

Josette kept wading, but she made slow progress because the rocks were slippery, and she didn't want to fall. Her feet got colder and colder. The bottom of her dress was wet and cold and flapped against her legs. She began to shiver. The trees cast shadows over the stream that no sun could shine through. Everything looked dark green and shadowy.

Josette kept on, hoping that she would soon reach the lake, but the water kept getting deeper until it was up to her knees. What if it got deeper that that? And deeper still? Where could she go? There was no shore, and just above her was the waterfall. She could never walk over the waterfall. It would hurl her back downstream.

For the first time, Josette was afraid.

When she took the next step, she could no longer feel the rocks of the streambed under her feet. Her feet were lifting her up into the stream. The water was deeper. She knew she had to turn back and return to the canoe. Her dress was wet and cold above her knees.

Finally she reached the canoe, sat down in it and rested in the warm sunshine.

Now she knew there was only one thing to do. She had to wait until the other canoe from the fort came to rescue her. There was still daylight, and it would stay light for a long time yet. The sailor had told her that at the tip of the Keweenaw Peninsula in June it stayed light until after 10 o'clock at night. There was still a lot of time for Edmund and his men to find her before bears or Indians did.

While she sat in the canoe, Josette began to feel sleepy. Her head nodded and her chin hit her chest. She stretched out sidewise in the canoe and let the sun shine on her wet dress and damp feet. She dozed and then fell asleep.

When she woke up, she didn't know how long she had slept. The sun was moving farther along in the sky. She was getting hungry and wondered what time it was. Then she heard gulls crying in the sky above her, a flock of them flying over the cove and over the canoe. They landed on Lake Superior close to the canoe, and one of them, a young one with brown feathers, flew into the canoe. He sat close to Josette, looking up at her.

"You're the gull that came to the ship," she said aloud to him. "I know you! You're the one I fed crackers."

The other gulls, the ones with gray feathers and golden beaks, landed on the water and started diving for fish, but the young gull stayed in the canoe with Josette.

She reached out and stroked his feathers. "I don't have any crackers for you," she said to him.

The gull just looked at her. He was not afraid.

"If you stay with me, I won't be afraid of being lost, or of bears, or of Indians," she said. "We'll wait together until Edmund comes." She paused. "And maybe you can come home with me and be my friend."

CHAPTER FOUR

making peace

When Edmund reached Captain Clary's quarters, the Captain greeted him warmly. "We can use an experienced man like you up here," he said. "Things are going well, but we need an officer to train the soldiers. "And," he added, "an officer who's interested in them personally. It's going to be a hard, lonely winter up here—and a long one. We want the men to stay healthy and reasonably happy."

"I'll do my best, Sir," Edmund said. "And I know my wife, Edith, and my sister-in-law, Josette, will help to make the soldiers feel at home. She'll be friends with everybody in a few days."

"We haven't seen any Indians yet," said the Captain. "That's why we're up here, you know, to protect the miners and their property rights, but that's good. We need the soldiers for our building projects. The soldiers and the civilians we hired are doing a great job together putting up the buildings. They've felled a lot of timber, and some of the men are working on the company quarters with mess rooms and kitchens adjoining. We want comfortable quarters for them. Next comes a storehouse for commissary and quartermaster.

The hospital building is finished, but we're waiting for plastering and painting. That should be ready in a week. Our doctor is coming on the next ship. We still have to build quarters for the laundresses, a blacksmith's shop, carpenter's shop, and last of all, stables for the horses. The sutler's shop is already up and running. The sutler, Charlie Brush, was appointed by William Wilkins, Secretary of War, the man the fort is named after. Charlie's doing a great job. He's filled his shop with goods to sell to the soldiers. I don't know how he lays his hands on eggs and butter, but he does."

"I smelled bread baking when I was walking over," said Edmund.

"Oh, yes, we have two soldiers who are good bakers. They supply us with fresh bread three times a day. The men hate hardtack. They call it 'worm castles,'" said the Captain.

Edmund told him how much he appreciated his quarters. "My wife and little sister-in-law are happy there. Tonight we'll eat our first supper together at our own table since we left our home in Virginia," he said. Then he asked the Captain about the troops.

"They're fine soldiers," the Captain said. "No soldier has been confined or arrested since we came, and even though the jail is ready, I hope it never gets any use."

The two officers talked about a number of things, but just before Edmund left the Captain said, "I'd watch over your little girl if I were you. Make sure she doesn't wander off the fort grounds. We do hear strange rumors about women and girls who have disappeared."

Edmund said he would report to the Captain in the morning, and on his way home he stopped at the sutler's store to pick up what food they would need for supper and breakfast. Tomorrow Edith and Josette could come to the store and buy what they needed for the days ahead. Edmund introduced himself to Charlie Brush, the sutler, and bought eggs, dried beef, cheese, butter, coffee, sugar and crackers. He knew how much Josette liked crackers. "I see you have a wife and daughter with you," said Charlie Brush.

"They'll be in to see you tomorrow themselves," said Edmund. "The little ten-year-old girl is my wife's sister. Her parents died, and she lives with us now."

"I'd be happy to serve them any time," said Charlie. "Maybe I can even find a few things that a ten-year-old girl would like for Christmas?"

"That would be wonderful," replied Edmund gratefully.

He walked back to where he had left Josette, on the lakeshore by the two canoes. He looked at his watch and saw that three hours had passed. Josette wasn't there any more. She must have gotten tired of waiting for him. Knowing Josette, Edmund was sure she had found things to do or soldiers to talk to. He didn't notice that one of the canoes was gone. When he stepped into the house, he called out, "I'm back, Edith."

"Is Josette with you?" his wife asked, coming to greet him.

"No, she isn't," he answered. "I thought she might be back here in the house with you."

"I haven't seen her since you both left three hours ago," said Edith.

"Maybe she's talking with the soldier standing guard. You know how she talks to everybody and makes friends. Since we left Virginia, she's made friends with a sailor, a miner, François and Private Wilks."

"Let's go and see," said Edith. "Or maybe she's

watching the men put up the company quarters. She might even be helping them."

Edith and Edmund went to talk to the soldier standing guard. "Have you seen a ten-year-old girl named Josette?" Edith asked.

"Not for a while," the soldier said. "I saw her standing by the lake, but that was some time ago. Can't you find her?"

"I left her at the lake about three hours ago," said Edmund, "but she's not there now."

"Nobody's got past me here," said the soldier. "Nobody went out, and nobody came in."

"Let's stop at the bakery," said Edith. "We need bread for supper, anyway. You haven't seen a ten-old-girl named Josette, have you?" Edith asked the baker.

"No," he replied, surprised at the question. "Is she missing?"

"We don't know," said Edmund, explaining that three hours ago he had left her beside the lake.

"She must be around here," said the soldier. "Would you like a loaf of bread for supper tonight?" he asked, handing Edith a fresh-baked loaf, still slightly warm.

"Thank you," said Edith, "and if you see Josette, will you send her home?"

"Yes, ma'am," he said, "and tomorrow I'll have a cookie ready for her."

Next Edith and Edmund stopped where men were working on a new building. Edmund asked one of them if he had seen a little girl or had talked with her.

"She's ten years old, and her name is Josette. She has long blonde hair. She was wearing a bonnet," said Edith.

"I'd know her if I saw her," the man said. "I'll ask Private Wilks if he's seen her."

Just then Private Wilks came around the corner of the building. "Have you seen Josette?" Edith asked him.

"That lovely little girl who rode with me this morning?" he asked. "Is she missing?"

"We don't know," said Edmund, "but we haven't seen her for about three hours."

"Sure hope nothing bad has happened to her," he said. "We hear stories about Indians and bears." Then he added, "If I can help search for her, let me know. I know the trail into Copper Harbor and all the other trails around here. I go hunting and fishing a lot."

"That's kind of you," said Edith.

They thanked him, hoping they wouldn't need a search party. "Let's go back to where you left her by the lake and see if there's any sign of her," said Edith.

When they got back to the lake, Edmund noticed that one of the canoes was missing. "I know there were two canoes here when I left her," he told Edith.

"She'd never go into a canoe on the lake by herself," said Edith. "She doesn't know how to paddle. She doesn't know how to swim!"

Edith started pacing back and forth. Her eye caught something in the canoe, and she walked back and looked more closely. Her heart fell. "Look, Edmund," she said, pointing to something white. "There's a bonnet in the canoe."

Edmund reached for the bonnet and handed it to Edith. "It's hers," said Edith.

"I don't think she'd take the canoe out all by herself," said Edmund.

"But if she's not in the missing canoe, where is she? And where is the canoe?" said Edith.

"Maybe one of the soldiers took her fishing," said

Edmund. "I'll ask whether any soldier had permission to go fishing."

Edith stayed at the lakeshore holding Josette's bonnet and the loaf of bread. She knew how much Josette loved fresh-baked bread still warm from the oven. She didn't want to ask herself if Josette had drowned or why the canoe was gone. She still hoped there was a simple answer to Josette's disappearance.

But when she saw Edmund walking back, she already knew the answer. No soldier was out fishing. Edmund said, "I think we'd better take this canoe out and search for her. I'll get Private Wilks to help."

Private Wilks came back with Edmund to the lakeshore where Edith was still waiting. "Don't you worry, ma'am," he said. "I know the lakes and streams up here. If you'll come with me, Sir," he said to Edmund, "we'll find her. If she drifted away in that canoe, I know where to look."

"And what if she's not in the canoe?" Edith asked anxiously.

"Then we'll organize a search party in the woods," Private Wilks said.

"Thank you," said Edith in a very low voice. She could hardly speak.

"Why don't you go back to the house and wait there," said Edmund. "We may be gone for some time. We want to find her before dark." Then he added, "Pray, Edith, and play the piano and sing some songs of hope."

"I will, I will," said Edith. She tried to smile. "I'll see you in a little while—with Josette." She walked slowly toward the house, scanning the fort in all directions.

Edmund sat in the bow and Private Wilks sat in the stern of the canoe, steering. "We'll turn left first," said Private Wilks. "That's a shorter distance. The lake ends up there in a channel that flows into a smaller lake. If she's there, we'll see her soon."

They paddled hard and soon came to the end of the lake. They saw immediately that Josette wasn't there. They paddled slowly in the shallow channel and came to a small, muddy lake. She wasn't there, either.

"Let's get out of this muddy lake and go to the other end of the first lake," said Private Wilks.

They paddled hard. The wind was with them, and Edmund kept looking along the edges of the lake on both sides to see if Josette might be there, but there was no sign of her or of the canoe. They saw a place where the bushes were trampled down. "Do you think she could be in there?" Edmund asked Private Wilks.

"That looks like a place where a bear came to the lake to fish," said Private Wilks. "I don't think we'll find her there. At least I hope not."

They paddled harder and suddenly found themselves turning and twisting, with the canoe swinging into a swiftly flowing stream. Before they knew it, they were plunging over a waterfall. "I hope she made it over this waterfall," Private Wilks called out to Edmund, but Edmund couldn't hear him over the roar of the water. Private Wilks steered the canoe so that they would avoid spilling over or hitting rocks. On both sides were steep cliffs. Then the canoe stopped, scraping bottom on gravel and shale. "We shouldn't be far from Lake Superior," Private Wilks said. He didn't say it, but he hoped that Josette wasn't adrift somewhere on Lake Superior. If she were, they'd never find her.

Suddenly someone was shouting to them. "You came, you came, you came! Here I am!"

"Josette!" Edmund and Private Wilks shouted.

They jumped out of the canoe. "You found me!" Josette cried happily, hugging them both.

"We're so glad to see you," said Edmund, hugging her tight.

Josette explained what had happened. It seemed like a long time that she had been here on the shore of Lake Superior, but her story was short—nowhere near long enough to confess how scared she had been.

"You did the best thing by staying with the canoe and not trying to find your way back," said Private Wilks.

"But I did try to find my way back," said Josette, and then she told them about the boulders on the shore of Lake Superior and about wading in the stream over her knees. "But how will we get back now?" she asked.

"We'll take you in our canoe, and then tomorrow I'll pick up yours with a couple of soldiers from the Fort," said Private Wilks.

They pushed the canoe off the bottom and started carrying it around the falls. "That falls must be about twenty feet," said Edmund. "Hang onto me, Josette, if the water gets too deep for you." Private Wilks guided them skillfully over the rocks, avoiding the deepest rushing water. Josette put her arms around Edmund's waist and clung to him until they got to the top of the falls. She was wet up to her chest, but she didn't care. She was safe at last.

The two men put the canoe on the lake and told her to get in the middle. They started paddling. Soon they reached the familiar lake, where the canoe slid easily over the water. They docked in front of Edmund and Edith's house, and Josette ran from the bank calling, "Edith, Edith!" Before she knew it, she was in Edith's arms.

"Oh, I'm so glad they found you!" Edith exclaimed. "Where were you?"

Josette didn't answer. "What about my friend, the gull?" Josette said. "I forgot all about him. He waited with me for you to come, and then I left him behind."

"You can tell me all about your canoe trip and your gull while we have supper," said Edith. "You must be very hungry."

"May Private Wilks have supper with us?" Josette asked.

"Of course," said Edith. "Run and invite him." Private Wilks was paddling the canoe with Edmund back to where it belonged on the shore.

Edith had a red-checked tablecloth on the table in the dining room. She had lit candles, and a lantern glowed on the mantelpiece. On the table she put fresh bread, butter, cheese, dried beef, crackers, coffee and a jar of strawberry jam she had brought from Virginia. Everyone agreed that this was the best supper they had ever tasted, and all during supper Josette talked about what had happened to her. But she didn't tell them about the bear and her cubs.

"Promise me you'll never get in a canoe again unless Edmund or Private Wilks is with you," said Edith.

"I promise," said Josette. "I was afraid I'd never see you again."

Edith turned her face away and got some more coffee. She didn't want to let Josette know how dangerous the canoe trip had really been. Josette might have drowned, Edith thought, close to tears, or been taken away by bears or Indians.

When they finished supper, Josette thanked Private Wilks again for rescuing her. She was so tired she went to bed immediately, but before falling asleep she remembered the young gull. She would ask Private Wilks in the morning to look for the gull when he went back for the other canoe. Maybe the gull would still be there, waiting for her. Then they could bring him back to her, and he could be her pet.

Just before she fell asleep (she didn't hear it), a bird landed on the roof of her house. It had brown feathers and a brown bill.

CHAPTER FIVE

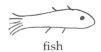

fish

The sound of a bird woke Josette up the next morning. It wasn't exactly a song—more like "Hiyah . . . hiyah . . . hiyah . . . yuk-yuckle-yuckle." Josette decided to get up and look around. She tiptoed past Edith and Edmund's bedroom, but Edith heard her. "Josette," she called out softly, "where are you going?" Edith was still worried about Josette after what had happened the day before.

"A bird woke me up. I think it's on the roof," whispered Josette. "May I feed it some crackers?"

"Yes, you may feed it some crackers, but don't go on the roof," said Edith. "I don't want you falling off."

By now Edmund was awake. "I'll make breakfast for us," said Edith. "Would you like eggs and toast?"

"I'll get fires started in the stove and in the fireplace," Edmund said. "But don't go far away, Josette. Stay where we can see you."

"I'll just go see the bird, and then I'll help with breakfast," Josette said. "I won't climb on the roof, and I won't go far away."

In the kitchen Josette found the crackers and put

them in her pocket. The bird's calling persisted: "Hiyah . . . hiyah . . . hiyah . . . yuk-yuckle-yuckle."

Outdoors Josette stepped back away from the house to look for the bird on the roof. It seemed to be a gull, a young gull. Could it be *her* gull? "I've got some crackers for you. Look," she called to him, holding out a cracker and waving it.

If he flew down to her, she'd be able to tell if he was her gull. She hoped he wouldn't be scared and fly away.

The gull flew down and landed at her feet. "It's you, it's you!" she shouted. "My gull, my friend!" She recognized him by the brown feathers and the shape of his brown beak. She held out a cracker to him. and he took it from her hand. Then another. "Stay here," she said to him. "I have to tell Edith and Edmund that you found me."

Edith and Edmund came out to look. The gull had stayed just where Josette had left him. They agreed with Josette. This had to be the gull that had befriended her on the ship and stayed with her when she was alone on the shore of Lake Superior. "Do you think we can keep him here?" asked Josette.

"I don't know why not," said Edmund. "As long as he has his freedom, there's plenty of fish here on the lake, and he's got you for a friend to feed him crackers. Why should he leave?"

"Let's have breakfast," said Edith. "The eggs are ready, and we can toast our bread over the fire."

"I'll see you in a little while," Josette said to the gull.

It was a delicious breakfast, they all agreed. They couldn't believe that Edith had made the eggs on the wood-fueled cookstove and that the bread hadn't burned when they toasted it over an open fire, and they couldn't believe that coffee made with clear lake water tasted so good.

Josette suddenly thought of something. "What shall I call him?" she asked.

Edmund joked with her. "You could call him 'Gullie' because he's a gull, or 'Herry' because he's a herring gull, or 'Freddie' because you remember Fredericksburg."

"I don't even think of Fredericksburg any more," said Josette. "I like it here. I think I'll call him Gullie."

Edmund pushed his chair back from the table. "I'll be gone for most of the day," he said. "I've got to talk to the soldiers about their duties. We have to establish good discipline so we can be ready if Indians attack. Though most of the men are busy building the fort, we must still have roll call three times a day, daily drills and parades, daily target practice and battalion, skirmish and bayonet drills. I'll read the *Articles of War* once a month, and I'll inspect the kitchen and bakery every day. A company that doesn't stay alert and in training isn't a good company."

"May I go see Private Wilks before you talk to the soldiers?" Josette asked. "I left some copper rocks in the canoe."

"That reminds me," Edmund replied. "Private Wilks and a couple of soldiers have to pick up that other canoe this morning. Come after the roll call and the drill, and you can talk to him about your copper rocks."

After Edmund left, Josette went outside to look for Gullie. He was floating on the lake, hunting for fish, so she went back into the kitchen to help Edith wash the dishes and make the beds. Before they could wash the dishes though, Josette had to go to the lake and fill a bucket with water. Then she went back and filled another bucket. All the water for the fort came from the lake and had to be hauled bucket by bucket. Josette went back for a third bucket of water to place next to the fireplace in case the fire got out of control.

When she had completed all her chores, she went to see if the men were finished with roll call and drill. She caught up with Private Wilks and Private Hawkins and two other soldiers just setting off in the canoe. "I left some copper rocks in the other canoe," she said. "Maybe they're valuable. Will you bring them back to me?"

"Yes," said Private Wilks. "We'll be back in an hour or two." A gull started swimming towards them. "Is that your gull?" Private Wilks asked.

"Yes," said Josette. "He found me. He's my best friend. My only friend," she added.

"I'm your friend, too," said Private Wilks. "How would you like to come to Copper Harbor with us later this afternoon to pick up some sheep? A ship is due in today to deliver them. We need fresh meat up here, and the sheep will be part of our meat supply, after they get fat on grass."

"Yes, yes," said Josette smiling. "Can we stop to see François, too?" She suddenly remembered that she'd have to get permission from Edith to go to Copper Harbor. "I'm sure Edith will let me go," she said.

"I'll stop at your house around four o'clock this afternoon with the wagon," said Private Wilks.

Josette ran to the house to ask Edith. "If you're going with Private Wilks, I won't worry," Edith said. "But for now, would you like to go shopping with me and carry some supplies back?"

They walked to the sutler's store and introduced themselves. "My name's Charles Brush," he said, introducing himself in turn, "but everybody calls me Charlie." Edith bought candles, soap, cheese, lard, flour, sugar, salt, tea, sauerkraut, pickles, syrup, dried apples, dried peaches and milk. Milk was hard to come by because there were so few dairy cows in the area, but that day Charlie had milk for sale, and Edith bought some for Josette. There were no fresh vegetables at all.

"The men are going to plant a vegetable garden about a mile from the fort," he said. "The ground here is too rocky. We'll see how the garden works out. We hope deer and rabbits won't eat the tender shoots of cabbage, spinach, carrots, turnips, and potatoes when they're just coming up."

Edith thanked the sutler, and then she and Josette went to the bakery. The soldiers greeted them, and one said, "I hear you've been riding the rapids, little girl."

Josette laughed. "I didn't fall out of the canoe when it flew over the falls," she said, "but I've promised Edith and Edmund not to try that again."

"That might be fun," said the other soldier. "I'd like to explore the lake and the stream some day."

"I saw a bear and her cubs," said Josette. She hadn't mentioned this before to Edith and Edmund.

Edith's eyes opened wide. "You saw a bear...?" her voice trailed off. One more thing to worry about!

"But I didn't see any Indians," she said. "Have you seen any?"

"Not yet," said a soldier.

"And we hope never," said the other.

The baker offered Edith a loaf of bread. "I'll save a loaf for you every day, if you'd like," he said. Edith was glad to hear that she wouldn't have to bake bread and that there would be fresh bread every day.

Josette looked around the bakery, but before she could see any cookies one of the bakers said, "We were saving something for you. How would you like a cookie?" He handed her a huge sugar cookie with a raisin on the top. "We baked a batch for dessert after dinner, but this one is especially for you."

"Oh, thank you," said Josette. "I'll see you tomorrow."

After Edith and Josette put away their food at home and ate a quick meal of bread and cheese and milk, Josette went outside to wait for Private Wilks. While she waited, she fed Gullie some crackers.

Before long Private Wilks, Private Hawkins and four other soldiers came by with horse-drawn wagons. "Are these your rocks?" Private Wilks asked her. Josette looked them over carefully.

"Yes," she said, counting them, "but there are two more here than I picked up. These other two are nicer than mine. I wonder who put them in the canoe?"

"Maybe a bear knew you were collecting rocks and added them to your collection," Private Hawkins joked. "Or maybe it was an Indian."

Josette was puzzled. "I'll leave them here under the seat until we get back," she said. She sat in front with Private Wilks. Riding through the woods reminded Josette of the day they arrived at the Fort. It seemed like a long time ago, but it was only yesterday!

When they reached Copper Harbor, Josette ran to the *Astor* to say hello to François. "My dear little friend," he said fondly, "you're back so soon."

"We're here to pick up some sheep," she said.

"Sheep? What will you do with sheep?" François asked.

"They're for fresh meat for the Fort," said Josette.

"Sheep graze on this rocky grass? Tough lamb chops! I have better meat here for you." He shook his head, muttering, "Sheep in these rocks!"

"I'll come back soon to eat some of your better meat," Josette promised. As she was saying "Goodbye," the ship was just docking.

Watching the ship being unloaded, Private Wilks told one of the sailors that he and the other men had come to pick up a couple of sheep for the Fort. "A couple?" responded the sailor. "More like twenty five."

Private Wilks looked at Private Hawkins. "We can't fit more than five in each wagon," he said. "That leaves fifteen to herd back to the Fort."

Josette counted the sheep as they stumbled off the ship. They had the same problem with their feet that she had had. The sailor was right, though. There were twenty-five sheep.

The soldiers managed to get five sheep into each wagon. The rest would have to walk. Four men were put in charge of herding the animals along the narrow path to the Fort. Private Hawkins drove the first wagon, then came fifteen sheep with soldiers on all sides of them, then came Private Wilks and Josette and five more sheep in the second wagon.

It was a slow procession. The sheep had been on board ship so long that they wanted to stop and graze every few steps. Some of them didn't want to walk at all. The soldiers prodded them gently. A few sheep wanted to wander farther into the woods to find fresh grass. The soldiers said they wished they had a sheep dog to keep the herd together.

Josette turned around to look at the five sheep riding with her and Private Wilks in the wagon. One of them came close to her and nibbled on her hand. "Baa-a-a," it said. "I think this sheep likes me," said Josette. "Do you think I could watch over her and keep her?"

"No harm in watching over her, I guess," he said,

"but she'll have to stay with the others, and once she's with the others, will you be able to tell which one she is? They all look alike to me."

The sheep "baa-a-ad" again and stayed close to Josette. "I can recognize her by her ears," said Josette. "One ear is much bigger than the other. When they're grazing at the fort, I'm sure I'll be able to pick her out."

"You can call her 'Mismatched' because her ears don't match," Private Wilks joked.

After a long, bumpy trip with many stops to herd the sheep back together, the two wagons and the herd arrived at the fort. The sheep that had ridden in the wagons were frisky when they were unloaded. The soldiers herded the other fifteen sheep inside the grounds of the fort, and the ten frisky wagon-riding sheep took the lead. Then something unexpected happened. When the soldiers tried to corral the sheep, the wagon-riders broke away and headed for the lake. They plunged into the lake and started swimming across it.

The soldiers didn't know what to do. They were stunned. They had never heard of sheep swimming. It took a few minutes before they realized they had to do something to bring the sheep back. But what could they do? By the time they gathered their wits, all the sheep were on their way to the south shore of the lake.

Hastily Private Wilks and Private Hawkins hopped in one canoe, and two other soldiers hopped in the other. They tried to head off the sheep, but the sheep kept on swimming. One fast-swimming sheep bumped into a canoe, almost tipping it over.

The sheep had already landed on the other side when the canoes finally made it to shore and herded together all those still standing on the shore. Five others were heading into the woods, and the soldiers shot them. They couldn't let their winter meat supply escape. Then they counted the sheep. There were fifteen, with five dead and five still missing. The soldiers decided not to hunt for the missing ones in the woods. They thought it would be best to herd the sheep into the lake, with one canoe leading them, acting like a lead sheep, and the other canoe following them, like a sheep dog.

When they landed on the shore of the fort, the soldiers were wet, but the sheep were dry because their thick wool shed water. Josette was waiting for them, and Edmund joined her. "Herd them into the open land next to the sutler's store," he ordered the soldiers. "I'll order men to build a temporary enclosure immediately. Otherwise we'll lose them again. How many are there?"

"Fifteen, Sir," said Private Wilks. "We had to shoot five on the other side, and five escaped. They went deep into the woods."

"We can probably send out a search party tomorrow," said Edmund, "and right now you can go back and pick up the five dead sheep. If we leave them overnight, wolves may get them."

Josette was looking at the fifteen sheep. She was afraid that her favorite was dead on the other side. She walked around the sheep while the soldiers herded them into the space being enclosed to keep them from swimming away again. One animal nudged her as they walked. She recognized the ears. My sheep is safe, she said to herself gratefully.

When Private Wilks and Private Hawkins returned once again to Fort Wilkins, other soldiers helped them carry the carcasses to the kitchen for butchering. The cooks welcomed the fresh meat. "We'll have a feast in a few days," one of the cooks said. "Chops, roast, stew! My mouth is watering just thinking about it."

Josette walked with the soldiers next to her sheep, Mismatched, while the enclosure quickly took shape. The sheep settled down and started nibbling on the grass that grew out of the rocky soil. Josette hoped her sheep would never turn into chops, roast or stew. She didn't know that in a few weeks the herd would nibble all the grass down to bare rock and that Edmund would have to find a pasture for her sheep and the fourteen others at least a mile away from the fort.

CHAPTER SIX

bear

The next few weeks passed quickly. June turned into July, and then it was August. Josette settled into a routine that included practicing the piano, reading and doing arithmetic problems. Edith wanted to make sure that Josette kept up with her music and her schoolwork over the summer, because when the baby arrived late in September, Edith would be too busy for a while to give Josette lessons.

Even with lessons and chores, though, there was still plenty of time each day for Josette to feed Gullie and to talk to him. Every morning he woke her up by sitting on the roof and calling "Hiyah . . . hiyah . . . hiyah . . . yuk-yuckle-yuckle." Then, after she had finished her music and schoolwork and helped Edith around the house, she walked over to the sheep enclosure and talked to Mismatched. Usually Mismatched was waiting for her by the fence of the enclosure.

Every day she went to see Private Wilks, also, after he got off duty. He asked her if some day she'd like to help him build a birchbark canoe. "Trouble is," he said, "I've got to meet an Indian first and get instructions on how to build a canoe before I can get started."

"I'll help you build the canoe," said Josette, "but where will we find an Indian?"

"We'll have to go into the woods for good birchbark," he said, "but we won't get lost. I know the woods pretty well by now. But where we'll find an Indian I don't know, unless François and the miners in Copper Harbor have seen Indians." He paused. "Do you like strawberries?" he asked Josette.

"Oh, yes," said Josette, "but where would we get strawberries? Does François have some?"

"I saw big patches of wild strawberries last night when I was in the woods scouting the birch trees for bark," he said.

"Where?" asked Josette.

"Right outside the fort on the Lake Superior side. I'll show you." Josette followed him just outside the Fort. "Look at these berries," he said, pointing to patches of wild strawberries. "Wouldn't they be nice for dessert tonight? I'm sure Mrs. Elliott would like some."

"I'll run and ask her if I may pick some," she said. "I'll have to go alone because my sister has trouble bending down now. The baby will be coming in a few weeks."

"If you stay close to the fort, you'll be all right," Private Wilks told Josette. "Just make sure stay close enough that you can always see the flag."

When Josette told Edith about the strawberries, Edith said, "It's a little late in the day to go strawberry picking, but strawberries would be nice for dessert and a change from all the dried fruit we've been eating. I don't like to have you go alone, though. Promise me that you'll stay within sight of the flag and that you'll get back long before dark."

Josette promised. She didn't want to get lost again.

Edith gave her a basket to hold the strawberries. "Remember," she said, "strawberries are delicate. Handle them carefully when you put them in the basket."

Josette went to the place Private Wilks had showed her. The ground was covered with brilliant red wild strawberries. Some were hidden in the grass so that the grass seemed to sprout red eyes. Josette bent down to pick strawberries. Just touching the berries made the juice squirt. She ate some before putting any in the basket, and they were so sweet and juicy that the juice stained her fingers and mouth. She squished them around in her mouth to make the juice last.

She soon discovered that the best way to pick strawberries was on her knees. She didn't mind if her dress got strawberry stains on it. She would worry about that later. After she had picked berries in the open spots, she moved to the berries in the taller grass, looking up to make sure she could still see the flag.

Ooh! In the tall grass the mosquitoes were fierce! They came in black clouds and bit her forehead and face. She had to loosen her bonnet and pull it down in front to protect her forehead and face and eyes. When she pulled her bonnet down, she got streaks of red strawberry juice all over it. She let the ribbons dangle loose.

After she picked a layer of strawberries, Josette put grass over them in the basket so that they wouldn't get crushed when she picked the next layer. She walked a little farther into the woods but forgot to look out for the flag as she walked. There were so many berries she ate a few more and sat down to rest. Birds were singing in the trees, and she could hear the gulls on Lake Superior. She thought she heard Gullie calling her from the roof of her house.

Gradually the woods lost some of its daylight.

Long shadows began to play on the trees. Josette's own shadow grew in the evening sunlight. She didn't notice three other shadows moving in her direction. There was one big one and two smaller shadows moving toward her and the strawberry patch.

She started picking again. It would take one more layer to have enough for supper because wild strawberries are small. When she stood up, she saw the grasses near her separating, and she stood still, wondering what could make grasses sway like that. Then she saw a bear moving through the grasses and heading straight for the strawberries. Two cubs followed the bear.

Josette didn't know what to do. There was no place to hide. Should she run, or should she walk backwards slowly? If she ran toward the Fort, she'd run right into the bear. He was on her path. If she backed into the woods, she'd get lost.

Suddenly Josette felt a tug on her dress. An Indian girl on her knees was pulling Josette away from the mother bear and her two cubs. The girl signaled for Josette to crawl, and Josette dropped to her knees and crawled as fast as she could behind the Indian girl. She dropped her basket. Her bonnet fell off, but she didn't notice because she was crawling so fast. Her bonnet landed in the deep grass.

The two girls crawled for a while. Josette looked back once or twice, and she could still see the bear and her cubs making their way to the strawberries, but she couldn't see the flag.

The Indian girl knew that a mother bear is able to smell humans and that a mother bear will do anything to protect her cubs from anyone who gets in their way. The Indian girl stood up and looked around. She motioned to Josette to stand up. There was no sign of the bears.

"Oh," said Josette, "I'm sure I'm lost. I'll never find my way back to the fort. I can't see the flag, and I lost my basket and bonnet."

"Come with me," said the Indian girl.

"You speak English!" Josette was surprised.

"I learned English from a priest at L'Anse. We live there in the cold months of winter," said the Indian girl.

"My sister will be worried about me," said Josette. "I live with her at the fort."

"I know that," said the Indian girl. "I like to watch you."

Josette felt afraid. The stories she had heard were true: Indians came to the fort and watched from behind the trees! She remembered how everybody had warned her that Indians would turn a little white girl into an Indian. She didn't want to spend the night with Indians in an Indian camp. Should she try to run away from the Indian girl? She didn't know which way to run. Besides, the Indian girl would be able to catch her in no time. She was older and taller than Josette.

"Come," said the Indian girl. "Don't be afraid." She looked deep into Josette's eyes. "You are afraid of me. I'll take you to the fort in the morning, but it's too late now. Now I'll take you to our camp. You will like my mother."

Josette knew that she had no choice but to go with the Indian girl. She could never find her way back. She was sure, though, that if she didn't return to the fort, Edmund and Private Wilks and the other soldiers would start looking for her. "Is your camp far away?" asked Josette.

"Not far," said the Indian girl.

They walked through the woods, not talking.

Josette had wanted to meet an Indian girl and talk with her, but now she didn't know what to say.

The Indian girl walked fast, ahead of Josette most of the time. She never looked back to see if Josette was still following her. Then she turned abruptly, near the tall mountain that Josette could see from the Fort, and Josette could hear a brook running. She could see fires burning. Then she was looking into an Indian camp. The Indians were burning damp grass that created a lot of smoke to keep the mosquitoes away.

The Indian girl led Josette to a wigwam where a woman was preparing supper. No men seemed to be around. The Indian girl said, "Mother, this is the white girl from the fort. Three bears were heading for her."

"You are welcome here," said the Indian mother. "Are you hungry?"

"Yes," said Josette. Then she added, "If I eat supper with you, will you turn me into an Indian forever?"

The Indian mother didn't answer Josette. Instead she asked her daughter, "Why did you bring her here? Why didn't you take her back to the fort?"

"I was afraid of the soldiers. I thought they might put me in their jail." The Indian girl didn't tell her mother that for a long time she had wanted a friend. There were no girls her age in the Indian camp, and she was often lonely.

"Now the soldiers at the fort will come looking for her," said the Indian mother, "and they will discover our camp."

"Will they hurt us?" asked the Indian girl fearfully.

"I have heard terrible stories about white soldiers," said the Indian mother. "They capture Indian girls and turn them into white girls and keep them forever."

Josette couldn't believe her ears. The Indians didn't want her in their camp. They didn't want to keep her forever. But the Indians believed that white soldiers captured Indian girls and changed them into white girls and kept *them* forever. Maybe the Indian girl wouldn't be allowed to take Josette back to the fort because of what her mother thought the soldiers would do to her.

Josette sighed. Now everybody was afraid. Maybe she would never see Edith and Edmund again.

"Mother," said the Indian girl, "is it time to eat?"

"Yes," said the Indian mother. "Let's not talk about being afraid. Let's make the little white girl feel at home."

"My name is Josette, and I'd like to eat with you," she said.

"My name is Maria," said the Indian girl.

The Indian mother got out some bowls of polished wood. Then she put something creamy yellow in the bowls. Then she poured maple syrup over the creamy yellow pudding. Finally she sprinkled strawberries over the top. Just watching the Indian mother cover the cornmeal pudding with maple syrup and strawberries made Josette feel at home.

"Thank you," said Josette. She and Maria sat down near the fire, away from the pesky mosquitoes, and ate their pudding. It was the most delicious pudding Josette had eaten since coming to the Fort. It made her mouth feel juicy. Her tongue lingered on the maple syrup. She pushed the strawberries up to the roof of her mouth and crushed them with her tongue. The juice gushed out. If the Indians could make pudding like this, Josette was sure that they didn't keep little white girls forever.

By the time the girls had finished their pudding, the men of the community came back. Josette didn't know where they had been. Had they been circling the Fort preparing to attack it? Had they been lurking in the shadows of the mines waiting to capture the miners when they came up?

Maria's father came to the wigwam. "This is Josette, Father," she said. "Three bears were getting close to her while she was picking strawberries, so I rescued her. She's from the fort."

He turned to his daughter. "Why did you bring her here?" he said.

"I was afraid to go to the fort," Maria explained.

"She is trouble for us," said Maria's father. "Soldiers will come looking for her. We don't want them to find our camp."

"I'll take her back as soon as it gets light," said Maria, "before they start hunting for her."

"That's too late," said her father. "I'll wake you up before sunrise, and we'll take her back together. Up to the place where she can find her way back. Not too close to the fort. We don't want the soldiers to see us."

"Come," said Maria's mother, smiling at Josette. "It's time to sleep. You sleep next to Maria."

Josette smiled back at Maria's mother. She felt close to Maria's mother. She was no longer afraid now that she knew the Indians didn't want to keep her forever. They didn't even want to keep her for the night, but they wouldn't abandon her. Alone she'd get lost.

The two girls lay down side by side. When they were almost asleep, Maria whispered to Josette, "I am glad that you are here. You are my friend." She squeezed Josette's hand.

"You are my friend, too," said Josette. I wish we could . . . " But before she could finish her wish, they had both drifted off to sleep. They were tired after that long walk.

In the night, Josette woke once. She heard howling. She thought it was wolves.

CHAPTER SEVEN

fear

Josette had been gone for over two hours, and Edith was getting worried Though she knew how small wild strawberries were and how long it took to pick a basketful, Edith thought that Josette should have been back by this time. She decided to walk to the edge of the woods where the wild strawberries grew. She wouldn't walk into the woods because she didn't want to fall and hurt herself or her baby, but she wanted to look in from the edge to see if she could catch sight of Josette.

Edith walked over to where she knew Josette had gone into the woods and put her hand over her eyes, squinting, trying to see deep into the trees. For a minute she thought she saw Josette's bonnet coming towards her, and she waved and called out, "Josette, Josette!" But it was only a wild daisy bending in the wind.

Edith paced back and forth between the edge of the woods and the grounds of the fort. Staring into the woods, she could see only white cedar trees and white birch trees. Where could Josette have gone? The flag flew so high over the fort that Edith was sure that it was clearly visible from a long distance, even if Josette had walked a little farther into the woods, she could still have seen it. She couldn't have lost sight of it, unless....

Then Edith did what most people do when they are worried about someone. She began to think of all the terrible things that could have happened to Josette. She thought of bears. Hadn't Josette seen a mother bear with two cubs on the lake, and didn't bears like strawberries? Could the bears have surprised Josette and.... Edith didn't allow herself to say the word "killed," even in her mind.

What else could have happened? The soldiers still talked about Indians spying on the fort at night. Had Indians been on the lookout for Josette and stalked her in the strawberry patch and... Edith didn't want to think the word "captured."

Or could Josette have forgotten about keeping within sight of the flag and simply walked too far away from the fort? If so, a search party would soon find her. Josette had already learned, from her experience on the lake, that the best thing to do when lost to was to stay in one spot, not to wander around and get even farther from your home.

Then Edith said to herself, I have to tell Edmund that Josette has disappeared so he can send search parties out to look for her.

She walked to the building where Edmund was just dismissing the soldiers from a meeting. She saw Private Wilks first. "Where's Josette?" he asked. "Is she still picking berries?"

"She hasn't come back yet," Edith replied, "and I'm worried. She's been gone for over two hours."

Just then Edmund appeared. Edith explained quickly about Josette. "Shall I organize search parties,

Sir?" said Private Wilks. "I feel partly responsible for telling her about the strawberry patches."

"Yes," said Edmund. "Let's go in as many directions as we can and cover a lot of ground before nightfall."

Private Wilks called a number of soldiers together. "Josette's missing again," he told them, "and we have to find her."

Everybody at the fort knew Josette and wanted to help search for her. "She can't be very far away if she's been gone only a couple of hours," said one of the soldiers. "We'll find her. Don't worry."

"I shouldn't have let her go," said Edith.

"It's not your fault," said Edmund. "We'll find her by the time you get supper on the table." Edith turned quickly and walked back to the house. She didn't want Edmund and the soldiers to see her tears.

The soldiers rounded up lanterns to light their way in case they had to search deep in the dark woods. Private Wilks mapped out directions. He would go with Edmund and two other soldiers to the place where Josette had been picking berries. Private Wilks knew that beyond the berry patches was a steep bluff. Josette might have stumbled over the edge of the bluff and fallen into the ravine below. If she had, getting down into the ravine would be a problem. Nobody mentioned aloud that the little girl might be seriously hurt.

A group of four other soldiers would take a path to Lake Superior to see if Josette had wandered down the shore and might be waiting for them to find her there.

Four more would go into the woods on the northeast side of the fort, taking the two canoes over the lake. That was the woods where the five sheep were still lost, even though several search parties had hunted for them, and one of the soldiers said that he could find his way around that area because he often took the canoe over the lake to hunt.

A fourth group of four would walk the trail to Copper Harbor to see if Josette had gone to visit with François while waiting to be found, and a fifth would search in the direction of a copper mine. Another fear no one mentioned aloud was that Josette might have fallen down an uncovered mine shaft. The miners often worked until dark and came back early in the morning when it was still dark, and sometimes they didn't cover the entrance to the mine.

Nobody mentioned Indians or bears aloud, either. All agreed to meet back at the fort in about an hour.

As they began their searches, they called Josette's name in every direction that they walked. "Josette, Josette!" One of the soldiers fired a shot in the air, thinking that Josette might hear it and come running out of the woods. The name "Josette" echoed all through the wilderness. Even Edith in her house heard "Josette! Josette!" But there was no answer.

Edmund and Private Wilks' search party started where they knew she had been picking berries, and the first patch they came to was well within sight of the flag of the fort. It looked like it had been picked clean by somebody who had knelt down in the grass to pick. It must have been Josette, but where did she go next?

They searched the ground carefully, looking for signs of Josette, for her footprints or for grasses that had recently been trampled. In a few spots, they thought they saw her small footprints.

As they walked farther, Private Wilks noticed that in several places the grasses had been flattened and trampled in a way that would have taken somebody much heavier than Josette. "Look here," he said, pointing to the flattened grass and crushed, glistening strawberries. "These are not signs of Josette."

"Bears?" Edmund asked. "Bears looking for strawberries? Do you think she was trying to escape from bears and ran away from them into the woods?"

"If so, let's hope she didn't rush over the bluff and fall into the deep ravine," Private Wilks said.

They searched a little farther, gradually approaching the bluff and ravine. Suddenly a soldier not far from the bluff called out, "Over here!"

The others rushed to him.

He was holding a basket. Someone shone a lantern on it. Picked strawberries were scattered on the ground nearby.

"It's Josette's," said Edmund. "She must have been running and tripped."

"At least we're on the right trail," said the soldier holding the basket.

"Let's search the ground on our way to the bluff and the ravine," said Private Wilks, "but be careful. We don't want anyone falling over the edge. It's a steep drop, and I don't know how we'd get anyone back out."

Then one of the soldiers saw something white in the deep grass. He picked up the object. He didn't want to call Edmund and the other soldiers over to see it, but he had no choice. "Over here!" he called.

They ran over and saw that he was holding a bonnet. Someone shone a lantern on it.

"It has red streaks all over it," Edmund said, taking the bonnet and stroking it. "It's Josette's." He could hardly talk.

"Looks like blood," a soldier said without thinking.

Why would there be blood on her bonnet? Edmund

wondered. He suddenly said, "Nobody would kill a beautiful little girl." He didn't even realize that he had said "kill."

"Those marks don't mean that she's dead," said Private Wilks. "They could just be strawberry stains."

"But why did she drop her bonnet if she weren't struggling to get away from somebody?" Edmund asked.

"Maybe she left it for us so that we could follow her trail, if she was running away from bears," said Private Wilks. "Let's see if we can pick up her trail."

They kept on in the direction of the bluff, shining their lanterns into the forest's obscurity, but they saw only trees and grass. Then one of the soldiers shone his lantern on something that looked like a large mushroom. As he got closer, he saw that it was a piece of cloth.

"Look here!" he called, picking it up. He handed it to Edmund.

"It looks like a piece of her dress," Edmund said. "It's one more sign that Josette has been here."

"Do you think she was crawling through here to escape the bears?" asked Private Wilks.

Edmund didn't want to go to the edge of the bluff and look down into the ravine, though all the signs pointed in that direction. He couldn't bear to think that Josette had fallen down the edge of the bluff. Would she be alive?

They reached the bluff, but they found no more pieces of Josette's dress and no other signs of Josette. They shone their lanterns down into the ravine, calling "Josette! Josette!" Their voices echoed, "'Ette, 'Ette" in the surrounding silence.

No one answered. If she had hurt her head falling down the ravine, though, Josette wouldn't be able to answer, Edmund reasoned. But as hard as they looked and swung their lanterns, they couldn't see anyone below the bluff, and they took that as a good sign.

By now it was getting dark in the woods. They had been searching for at least an hour, and it was time to get back to the fort. "There's not much more we can do until morning light," said Edmund.

"Do you think, Sir, that one of the other search parties has found her?" one of the soldiers asked.

"I'm not hopeful," said Edmund, "but maybe she did make her way to François."

On the way back nobody talked. Edmund carried Josette's basket, her bonnet, and the piece of her dress.

When they got back to the fort, the other search parties were waiting for them. Josette wasn't there. The soldiers who had taken the canoes over the lake were standing there smiling because they had five sheep with them. They had found the sheep that were lost in the woods.

When Edith saw Edmund and the soldiers, she came running out of the house, and then she saw that Edmund was holding a basket. "Oh, Edmund," she cried.

"We found her basket," said Edmund. "That's a good sign. We know that she was picking berries there before she disappeared."

"What else did you find?" asked Edith.

He handed her the bonnet.

"It's covered with blood!" she cried. She dropped the bonnet as Edmund reached out to keep her from falling, and she fainted.

When Edith revived, Edmund tried to reassure her. "It's not necessarily blood," he said. "Private Wilks thinks it's only strawberry juice."

Edith said, "But where is she?"

"We don't know," said Edmund, "but if she crawled away from bears, she's got to be somewhere in the vicinity."

"Crawled away from bears?" asked Edith. "How do you know she was crawling? Did you see bears?"

"No," said Edmund, "we didn't see bears, but we saw signs of bears in the strawberry patches. We think she was crawling away because we found this." He hadn't planned to show Edith the piece of torn cloth from Josette's dress they had found, but he thought she should be prepared for anything they might discover the next morning. "Here," he handed her the torn cloth.

"That's from Josette's dress," said Edith. "She's dead, I just know it."

"No," all the soldiers shouted, "we're not giving up!"

"If she were dead, we would have found her body," added Private Wilks.

"Let's all get a good night's rest," Edmund said to the soldiers. "We'll sound reveille with fife and drum for 5 o'clock tomorrow morning and pick up where our search left off. And thank you, all."

The soldiers said they were eager to resume the search in the morning. They said good night and went quietly to their quarters. Those who had found the five sheep herded them into the enclosure with the fifteen others. One sheep in the enclosure sidled up to the fence. She seemed to be waiting for somebody.

"She's alive," said Edmund to Edith as they walked back to the empty house. "I know she's alive."

Edith said, "I'll pray that she's all right wherever she is. Even if Indians have found her."

CHAPTER EIGHT

teepee

Josette woke before sunrise, and at first she couldn't remember where she was. Then she saw Maria sleeping next to her and remembered that an Indian girl had rescued her from bears. Josette got up quietly and crawled to the opening of the wigwam. She wondered whether she could find her way back to the fort alone when daylight came. She still wasn't sure about Indians and began to have doubts about Maria. Was Maria really the good friend she pretended to be? Or were the soldiers right about Indians?

She crawled out of the wigwam and stood up. Stars were still shining above, and she thought she was the first one up in the camp until she heard, "Good morning, Josette." Maria's father had come up behind her so quietly she hadn't heard him. There was no chance of escaping, she thought.

"Can I go back to the fort now?" she asked.

"We'll have some breakfast first," said Maria's father.

Another postponement, Josette thought. Was this a way of keeping her here forever?

Maria came out of the wigwam, saying, "I'm ready

to go," and Josette knew when she heard those words that Maria could be trusted.

"We must first give breakfast to your friend," said Maria's mother, coming out of the wigwam. "It is a long walk back."

Josette liked the way Maria's mother said "your friend." Maria's mother boiled water over a fire and made blackberry tea. She sweetened it with honey, and it tasted good in the cold morning air. Next she gave them bowls of dark rice with maple syrup on top. The maple syrup sank into the rice and made it sweeter and moister than any rice Josette had ever eaten. Before they left, Maria's mother gave Josette and Maria a lump of maple sugar. "It's to eat on the way," she said.

"Come," said Maria's father. "It is getting late. I had a dream last night that the soldiers from the fort were searching for you. I do not want to meet them."

"They wouldn't hurt you," said Josette.

"They hurt all Indians," said Maria's father. "They have guns, not for hunting but to kill us. They took away all our land and filled it with holes. Miners are crawling over our land and scaring away animals. Now we cannot hunt here. We have to go far away to hunt."

For a while they walked in the faint light of dawn. Maria and her father walked so fast that Josette could hardly keep up with them. Their feet seemed to glide over the rocks in the earth while her toes kept bumping into rocks, and her feet kept tripping over sticks and tree roots.

The stars disappeared. Birds started singing. The air was filled with morning sounds. The sky turned gray, then blue, then pink. Soon the sun would come up as a big red ball. "Hurry," said Maria's father.

"How can you find your way?" Josette asked. "All

the trees look the same to me. I would get lost without you."

"We have lived here a long time," said Maria's father. "We are Ojibwe. We learned from our fathers."

"And from our mothers," added Maria.

"Do you kill white men?" asked Josette.

"No," said Maria's father. "We kill only deer and bear and animals for food and for skins." He paused. "But white men kill Ojibwe for fun."

"No, they don't," said Josette. "They don't even know what you look like."

"Then why do they have guns? Why do they build a fort?"

Josette did not know the answers to his questions. She knew that the soldiers were always talking about Indians because they were afraid of them. "If you come to the fort with me," she said, "they will not shoot you."

"I do not trust the white soldiers," said Maria's father. "They like only dead Indians."

"My sister would like you, and so would Edmund. He's second in command at the fort."

Then Maria spoke. "Father," she said, "may I go with Josette to tell her sister and her brother that we will not harm them?"

"No," said her father. "They would keep you in the fort. Then we would have to fight to get you back."

"No," said Josette. "Maria is my friend. She is my *only* friend. They would like her."

"They would like her too much. They would turn her into a white girl," said Maria's father.

"But, Father, I would like to visit the fort. And I would like her to come back to our camp. I have no friends," said Maria.

"That is not possible," said Maria's father.

Suddenly he stopped. He motioned to them to be quiet. He listened. He heard something. He dropped to the ground and was completely covered by tall grass. Maria and Josette dropped down beside him. He put his ear to the ground. He put his fingers to his lips, "Shh—," he whispered.

"What is it?" Maria whispered.

"Soldiers?" Josette whispered.

He did not answer. Then he held up one finger. Then another. Then another. "One big bear," he said, "and two little ones."

"Are they looking for me?" asked Josette.

"No," said Maria's father. "This is their territory. They stay. We go."

He got up. Everything was all right. They could go on.

They continued on their way. Soon they would be close to the fort. The sun was not up yet, but it was light enough now to see where they were.

"I know where I am," said Josette suddenly. "I can find my way now." They could see the smoke of fires at the fort.

"Now you go," said Maria's father. "Do not tell them where our camp is."

"Oh, I won't," said Josette. "I couldn't find it again, anyway. But thank you for taking care of me last night."

Then Josette turned to Maria. "Will you come again to the fort? We could go berry picking together. Then I won't get lost."

"I could teach you many things," said Maria.

"I can meet you at the berry patch where you found me," said Josette.

Maria laughed. "I could save you again from bears."

"We must go now," said Maria's father. He started walking away.

"I'll come to the berry patch close to the fort tonight," whispered Josette.

"Hurry," said Maria's father, "before the soldiers see us and start shooting."

"I'll meet you there," Maria whispered back.

"When you come," said Josette, "whistle like a white-throated sparrow. Then I'll know that it's you."

"Here," said Maria, handing Josette the piece of maple sugar that her mother had given her. It was a lovely gift from a friend. Then Maria and her father were gone, blending into the white cedar trees and the white birch trees and the giant pines and the tall grasses.

Josette ran. She wanted to surprise Edith and Edmund. By the time she reached the boundaries of the fort, though, soldiers on guard had spotted her. They shouted, "Josette is safe! Josette is safe!" One soldier rang the bell. Another shot a gun into the air. Gullie screeched from the rooftop, "Hiyah . . . hiyah . . . hiyah . . . yuk-yuckle-yuckle."

Edith and Edmund came running out of their house. They had not slept all night. "Josette," said Edith, "Josette!" Edith hugged Josette as best she could. And then Edith said, "We thought you were dead."

"The Indians—" began Josette.

"What Indians? Did they capture you?" asked Edmund.

"No," said Josette, "they saved me."

"How did you get mixed up with Indians?" asked Edmund.

"We thought you'd been scalped," said Edith. "There was so much blood on your bonnet."

"Blood?" said Josette. "Blood?" Then Josette laughed. "That was strawberry juice!"

"Did you see any Indians with scalps on their belts?" Edith asked.

"No," said Josette. "Everybody was nice to me. Maria's father didn't have any scalps on his belt."

"He probably hid the scalps when you were there," said Edith.

Edith wanted to hear all about the Indians and why Josette had disappeared for a whole night. "Let's have breakfast, and then we can talk," she said.

"I had breakfast," said Josette. "Rice with maple syrup."

"We found your basket of berries," said Edmund.

"Did you eat them?" Josette asked.

"I couldn't swallow a single berry," said Edith. "Not while you were missing."

"Let's eat them now," said Josette. "I hope there are enough left in the basket. I dropped it when I was trying to escape from bears." She explained about the bears and about the Indian girl who had rescued her and brought her to their camp.

"I want to see Maria again," said Josette. "I like her mother and her father, too. She is my friend."

"You must never get near an Indian again," said Edmund. "They're dangerous. Even Indian girls are dangerous."

Josette didn't say anything. She knew Edmund was wrong. She didn't tell them that she had promised to meet Maria again that very evening.

Josette and Edith spent the rest of the day talking and resting. They were both tired. Josette tried to tell

Edith how kind the Indians were, and Edith began to believe her. "It would be nice to talk to Maria's mother," said Edith, "but I don't know how we'd arrange it. The soldiers don't want any Indians on the grounds of the fort, or anywhere near the fort."

That night after supper Josette said, "I'm going to talk to the soldier on guard. I want to tell him about my Indian friend."

"Just stay close to the fort," said Edmund. "Those Indians may be coming back for you."

Josette didn't say that one of the reasons she wanted to go talk to the soldier on guard was to listen for Maria. She told the soldier the story about her escape from the bears and about her rescue by an Indian girl named Maria. "I'm glad to see you got back unharmed," he said, "but remember, you can't trust an Indian."

"Or a bear," said Josette.

Just then she thought she heard the song of a white-throated sparrow. "Peabody-Peabody-Peabody!" Then she heard it again. "Peabody-Peabody-Peabody!" This time the song was closer.

"I'll just walk a little way," said Josette. "Where you can see me."

Josette walked to the entrance of the woods where she had first picked strawberries. "Peabody-Peabody-Peabody!"

"Maria," she called. "Are you there?"

"Yes," called Maria. "Come a little closer to the strawberry patch."

Josette didn't dare to go very far into the woods because she knew the soldier on guard was watching her. She waved at him, and he waved back. She pointed to him that she was going in—just a little way—and he waved again, signaling that he understood.

"Here, Josette," called Maria from behind a tree. Maria moved closer so that Josette could see her.

Josette ran towards Maria. "You came!" she said happily. "You're my true friend." Josette wanted to know all about Maria and the Indians. "Where do you come from?" she asked.

"From here," said Maria. "This is our home and our land."

"Didn't you ever live anyplace else?" asked Josette.

"Just when we go on hunting trips and when we live in L'Anse in the deep snows of winter," said Maria. "Where do you come from?"

"Virginia," said Josette.

"Where is Virginia?" asked Maria.

"Over the water and by train," said Josette. "About a thousand miles."

"Are there Indians in Virginia?" asked Maria.

"A long time ago," said Josette, "but I've never seen an Indian there."

"Am I the first Indian you ever saw?" asked Maria.

"Yes," said Josette, "and you are the best friend I ever had."

"You are my best friend, too," said Maria. "I wish we could live together."

"So do I," said Josette, "but the soldiers are afraid of Indians. Even Edith is afraid."

"Afraid of me, a twelve-year-old girl?" said Maria.

"Maybe they won't be afraid if you come to the fort with me," said Josette. "Come." She held Maria's hand and led her toward the soldier on guard.

The soldier was surprised to see another girl with Josette. "This is my friend Maria," Josette explained. "I want her to meet my sister. Maria is the girl who saved my life."

The soldier smiled at Josette. He didn't see anything wrong with letting Edith meet the girl who had rescued Josette, even if she was an Indian. Maria breathed a sigh of relief that the soldier hadn't aimed his gun at her.

When Edith, who was sitting on the veranda, saw Josette with an Indian girl, she called out, "Welcome, Maria!"

Maria smiled and said hello.

"You are always welcome here," said Edith. "Thank you for saving Josette's life."

"May Maria come back tomorrow?" asked Josette. "She can teach me many things."

"Yes, of course," said Edith. "Maybe your mother would like to come, too, Maria. There are many things she can teach me about having a baby here in the wilderness."

"I must go now," said Maria, "or my mother will be worried."

"All mothers feel the same," said Edith, "and even big sisters worry."

Josette walked with her friend to the entrance of the fort. She waited with the soldier on guard until Maria disappeared into the woods. Then, just as Josette was about to walk back to the house, she heard "Peabody-Peabody-Peabody!"

"That's the second time I've heard the white throated sparrow tonight," said the soldier. "He sounds close."

Josette smiled.

CHAPTER NINE

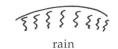

rain

All that night a heavy rain driven by high winds battered Fort Wilkins, but Josette didn't hear the rain rattling her window. She didn't hear waves slapping the rocks on Lake Superior, spraying the shore and driving gulls and ducks into coves for shelter. Josette was fast asleep. After the excitement of her encounter with a mother bear and two cubs, then an overnight stay in an Indian camp, she was exhausted. Edith didn't wake her. Edith and Edmund ate breakfast without her.

The sun didn't come up that morning at Fort Wilkins. The sky was dark gray, and clouds hung low over the fort. Gullie didn't sit on the roof and call her. He was hiding in a little sheltered cove on the lake.

Josette didn't hear the sounds of soldiers in their morning drill. They couldn't drill because of the soaking rain. Edmund was inside with them giving them other duties that could be performed indoors. The only soldiers outside in the rain were those on guard.

Water puddled between the rocks and flooded the lower grounds of the fort, washing away the topsoil. The sheep were safe because they were in an enclosure on higher ground.

As Josette was beginning to come out of her sleep but before she was completely awake, she had a morning dream. She dreamed that she was picking strawberries and that three bears were approaching her. In her dream she could feel an Indian girl pulling her down and telling her to crawl. When she started to crawl, she woke up on her knees, halfway out of her bed. She suddenly realized that she was in her own bedroom and not in a strawberry patch.

She jumped up and looked out the window, remembering that Maria had promised to come back today. They had so many things to talk about! But Josette couldn't see out the windows. The rain blurred all the buildings at the fort. Rain blocked out the bakery and the sutler's store, her two favorite places. She wanted to take Maria to them and maybe get a cookie for Maria and herself.

She ran down the steps to the kitchen calling to Edith, "It's raining so hard, Maria won't be able to come today."

"Good morning," said Edith. "Maybe the rain will stop by noon and she'll come this afternoon or tonight." Edith was trying to cheer Josette up. "Now let's get some breakfast into you."

While Josette ate breakfast, she asked Edith questions that were troubling her. "Do you think Maria will really come to see me after the rain stops? Do you think her father will let her come to the Fort?"

"She came last night," said Edith. "That should reassure her father that nobody at the fort will harm her."

"Would you let me go back to the Indian camp with Maria?" Josette asked. "Would you trust the Indians not to keep me?"

Those were hard questions for Edith to answer, as the first ones would be hard questions for Maria's parents to answer. Edith didn't want to lie to Josette. Instead she said, "Maybe we could invite Maria and her mother and father to have supper with us."

"I wish her mother and father would come," said Josette. "Her father could teach Private Wilks how to build a birchbark canoe. But how can we invite them if we don't know where their camp is?"

Edith said, "If Maria said she was coming, I'm sure she'll keep her promise, and then we can give her the invitation to her mother and father to have supper with us."

Edith wasn't at all sure that she should have said this, but she hoped with all her heart that Josette wouldn't be disappointed. Edith knew that it would be unusual to have Indians come for supper at the fort. She knew the soldiers and miners didn't look kindly on Indians, even though they had never seen any. Maybe the Captain wouldn't allow Indian guests. Edmund was here to protect the miners from attacks by Indians. How would he feel about having Indians in their house? How would his men feel about it?

Edith didn't tell Josette about the Indians on Isle Royale out in Lake Superior about fifty miles from Copper Harbor. Edmund had told her that those Indians were refusing to give up their land to miners who could show claims to the land. Even though the Indians had signed treaties with the United States government, they didn't want to be pushed off the land that had been theirs for centuries.

Edith had also heard from Edmund that when miners were blasting into rocks and making shafts for their mines, they had discovered 3,000 year old pits. No one could believe that Indians had discovered copper long before white miners had come to Copper Harbor, but they couldn't deny the evidence. How could Indians mine copper without modern tools? They had dug up tons of it with only fire, cold water, and stone hammers. Indians might want to do copper mining again, and that threatened the miners who were hoping to make a fortune on copper.

Edith thought of something to console Josette. "There's a saying that a person who saves someone's life feels attached to that person for the rest of her life. That's how Maria will feel about you."

"Even if that person is an Indian who has saved a white girl?" asked Josette.

"Especially if that person is an Indian who has saved a white girl," said Edith.

The rain did not stop by noon. It stopped only in the middle of the next night when Josette was again asleep. When she woke the following morning and got up to look out the window, she saw a world shrouded in fog. Fog rubbed against the window. It blotted out the fort. She could not see the lake. She couldn't hear Gullie's song. Was he lost in the fog? Thinking about Maria, Josette's heart sank. Maria couldn't come today, either.

The fog lasted for three days. No one came into the fort, and no one went out. Edmund could hardly make his way to the men's quarters. He didn't want Edith or Josette to go outdoors for fear they might get lost or bump into a tree or fall into the lake.

Then gradually the fog lifted a little. The two soldiers who were assigned to find wild game went hunting for fresh meat. In the fog about a hundred yards from the fort, one of them stumbled and almost fell. When he looked down at what he had tripped over, he saw something gleaming in the fog. He and the other soldier got down on their knees to uncover the rest of what was shining up at them, and as they rubbed their hands over it, they saw that it was copper. It was a dazzling sight, spread all over on the top of and inside the crevices of a huge rock. They realized that this must be a rich deposit of copper not yet discovered by the miners.

By this time the fog had lifted above the tops of the trees, and one of the soldiers said, "I'll go back and tell Lieutenant Elliott. You stay here so that we can find it again."

Not long after, he walked to the gleaming rock with Edmund. Edmund said that this was the brightest copper he had ever seen and might be a good site for a mine. He said, "Let's put a marker here so that can find it again. I'll go into Copper Harbor and tell the mine owner that we met on the boat about it. Josette has his name."

As Edmund came back to the house, he called out, "Josette, do you still have the name of the mine owner that you met on the boat? The one with the birchbark scroll with Indian writing on it?"

Josette came dashing out to meet Edmund. "I've got it in my top bureau drawer," she said. "I'll get it."

Edith joined them. "Why do you want the miner's name?" she asked.

"We think we've found a rich copper deposit about a hundred yards from the fort. Two soldiers stumbled on it. I want to talk to the mine owner about it," said Edmund.

"Here's the name," said Josette, reading it as she ran toward Edmund, "John Hayes. Is he going to dig a mine close to the fort? Then I can watch!"

"Hold on there," said Edmund. "I'm not sure yet. But that rock looks like it's hiding a lot more copper under it."

"Are you going to Copper Harbor now to talk to him?" Josette asked.

"Yes," said Edmund. "Do you want to come along? The fog has cleared, and we'll ask Private Wilks to drive us on the wagon."

Josette suddenly thought about Maria. "What if Maria comes," she asked Edith, "and I'm not here?"

"I'll meet her," said Edith, "and have her wait with me until you get back."

"I'll have to tell you our secret call so that you can find her," said Josette. "She whistles 'Peabody-Peabody-Peabody' like the white-throated sparrow, just at the entrance to the strawberry patch."

"Don't go into the woods," said Edmund to Edith. "You don't want to fall."

"I'll wave a white dish towel at the entrance to the woods," said Edith. "Then she'll know I'm there."

"I'll be back with Private Wilks in a few minutes," said Edmund. He could hardly hide the excitement in his voice. "Bring along the slip with the miner's name on it, and we'll find him in Copper Harbor."

As they rode the narrow track into Copper Harbor, the wagon narrowly escaped getting stuck in the mud, but Private Wilks was a skillful driver, and he avoided puddles and holes. When they arrived in Copper Harbor, Edmund decided that the best place to go was to the *Astor* where François worked, since François knew every miner in the vicinity.

François was happy to see Josette. "My little flower," he said, "you come back to see me! To eat?"

Edmund explained that they were looking for John Hayes, the owner of a mine.

"Yes, I know him," said François. "He lives in the big log house. I show you." François stepped outside and pointed to the biggest log house in Copper Harbor. "I think he is there now. He comes here about one o'clock for dinner."

"Thank you," said Edmund. "We'll find him and come back and have dinner with him."

Before they even reached the door of the log house, John Hayes stepped out to greet them. He had seen Josette and recognized her from the ship. "My little friend," he said, "you have come to see me."

Josette said, "I saved the paper with your name on it, and that helped Edmund find you." She smiled warmly at him.

Then Edmund told him about the discovery of copper by two soldiers. He explained that it was outside the boundaries of the fort and that he wondered whether John Hayes would be interested in looking at it.

"I'm definitely interested," said John Hayes. "Let's have dinner and then we can talk about possibilities."

François served all the good things he always served, but for Josette he had a special treat. "This meat is not mutton. It is very tender," he said. "You guess what it is." He put a piece of white meat on her plate. The white meat was so tender she could cut it with her fork. "You like?" he asked her.

"Good," she said. "Very good." She ate faster than she usually did, it was so delicious. After she had finished the meat, she said, "I guess—pigeon!"

"Duck," François said, "basted in wine."

During dinner Edmund learned that John Hayes was from Pittsburgh and had come to Copper Harbor in the spring, just before the soldiers arrived to establish Fort Wilkins. Hayes explained that his men were now working on two mines close to Lake Superior, almost opposite the fort, down where the land curved to enclose the bay. He was eager to see the rock that the soldiers had stumbled on. After dinner he said he would go to his house to pick up some equipment for examining the site.

Josette suddenly remembered the birchbark scroll. "Do you still have the Indian scroll?" she asked him.

"Oh, yes," he said, "I'll get that, too, and you can look at it when we get to the fort."

"I have an Indian friend now," said Josette, "maybe she can help us read the pictures."

"I'd like to meet her," said John Hayes.

"Maybe she'll be at my house when we get back," said Josette.

On the way back to the fort, John Hayes explained copper mining to Edmund. He said that gunpowder was used to blast an opening into hard rock and that most of the mineshafts were about five feet wide by seven feet long. His men blasted as deep as was necessary to extract the copper from the rocks, mostly about 40 feet deep into the earth. These were small mines, he said. He dreamed of finding copper in the mountains that formed the spine of the Keweenaw peninsula, of digging deep into the earth and fanning out in miles of underground tunnels, where they could go down as deep as twelve levels. But that would take engineering skills. Right now, near Copper Harbor, the mines were small but good sources of copper. Mr. Hayes told Edmund he was getting about eighty percent copper out of black oxide and was particularly happy to find native copper in rocks close to the surface.

Josette listened carefully. She hoped that he would allow her to watch them bringing up copper. Maybe they would even let her go down in the mine. She wondered what it would feel like to go forty feet under the ground.

By the time they got back to the fort, Josette couldn't wait to see if Maria had come. "Here," said John Hayes, "you take the birchbark scroll with you and show it to your Indian friend. I'll go with Lieutenant Elliott to see the copper rock. We'll see you later." He handed her the scroll. She could hardly believe that she was holding something so old, left in a cave by Indians long ago.

She ran to the house and called, "Edith, I'm back!" When she stepped into the kitchen, there was Edith, serving tea and cookies to Maria and her mother!

"You came!" Josette cried happily. "I knew you would."

"Sit down and have tea and a cookie," said Edith. "Then you and Maria can talk, and I can visit with Maria's mother."

Josette was so excited that she ate her cookie fast, even though she usually liked to eat such a special treat slowly. "Look," she said to Maria after she had finished her tea and cookie. "The mine owner, Mr. Hayes, gave me this to show you." She handed Maria the scroll.

Maria showed it to her mother. "This is an Ojibwe scroll," said Maria's mother. "Pictographs. Picture writing. We still write in pictures. We do not write our own word language, we only speak it. I will look at this more carefully after Edith and I talk about babies."

Josette took Maria up to her room and opened her top dresser drawer. She took out her collection of copper rocks. She told Maria about how she had gotten lost in a canoe on the lake and on the stream and had landed on the shore of Lake Superior her first day at the fort. Then she showed Maria the copper rocks she had picked up along Lake Superior. "But here are two extra rocks that I didn't find," Josette said. "I don't know who put them in the canoe for me."

"I know who," said Maria with a smile.

CHAPTER TEN

talk together

When Josette and Maria went back downstairs to look at the birchbark scroll, they found Edith and Maria's mother in the middle of a serious conversation about the birth of a baby. Josette and Maria listened to what the women were saying. Maria's mother said that she was trained in Indian medicine to help deliver a baby and that she would come to help if Edith needed her. Edith said that Dr. Isaacs, the doctor at the fort, had promised to help deliver the baby when the time came. Maria's mother said, "I have delivered Indian babies, and not one mother or baby died."

Edith looked troubled. Before leaving Virginia and coming to the wilderness on the shores of Lake Superior, she had worried about having a baby so far from medical help. She had been reassured when meeting Dr. Isaacs, who told her that he had delivered many babies on Army posts on frontiers. He told her not to worry. But now when she heard the word "die" from Maria's mother, she felt her old worries coming back. What if the baby came early and Dr. Isaacs wasn't at the fort?

Josette couldn't bear the thought of Edith or her

baby dying. "Could we look at the scroll now?" she asked to change the subject.

"Of course," said Maria's mother. She unrolled the scroll carefully, and the others looked over her shoulder. The scroll was filled with pictures that seemed to tell a story. After studying each pictograph, Maria's mother said, "I cannot read these pictures, but Maria's father can. He is an expert in Ojibwe picture writing."

"Will he come to the fort?" Josette asked, adding, "and will he eat supper with us?"

"I'll persuade him," said Maria.

"He will have to be assured that the soldiers will not take him prisoner. They might think that he's an Indian spy, come to find out how many soldiers are here," said Maria's mother, "and how many guns. He will be afraid that they will think that and put him in jail."

"I won't let that happen," said Edith. "I'll talk to Edmund, and he'll make sure that Maria's father will not be harmed by the soldiers."

"We shall see if he will come," said Maria's mother. Turning to the girls, she said, "I cannot read the pictures in the scroll, but I can draw other pictures for you. Then you can learn about the pictures we use today."

Josette quickly got a piece of paper for her and a pen and ink. Maria's mother began to draw a picture.

"Can you guess what this is?" Maria's mother asked.

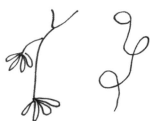

"Plants?" they asked. "Flowers?"

"Plants that cure people," said Maria's mother. "I will use these plants when Edith's baby comes."

She began to draw another picture.

Josette and Maria couldn't decide what that picture meant. After looking at it carefully, Josette asked, "Is it a man?"

"If it is a man, what is he holding?" Maria asked.

"It is a man," said Maria's mother, "and he is holding a gun. This is the picture that Maria's father draws in the camp and shows to all of us. It is a soldier at the fort holding a gun and trying to destroy us."

"Oh, no," said Edith. "The soldiers are here only if Indians attack the miners."

"We fear that soldiers will kill us," said Maria's mother.

They were all silent. Josette wanted the talk of dying and killing to stop. She took Maria's hand in hers and said, "We are friends. Maria saved me from bears. And now you are here to help us. The soldiers at the fort will not kill you. The soldiers are good men."

"Can you draw a happy picture, Mother?" Maria asked.

Maria's mother began to draw again.

No one could guess what the picture said.

"The top lines are the sky," said Maria's mother. "Underneath the sky is a spike of mullein. That is a plant that has a big spike with yellow flowers. We take the spike and dry it. Then we light it like a candle. In the picture it has fire coming out of it. Now can you guess what it means?"

They shook their heads. What could a sky with a mullein plant that was burning like a candle mean?

Edith looked thoughtful. "Does it mean prayer?" she asked hesitantly.

"Yes," said Maria's mother. "The fire means that we pray to Someone above us. Sometimes we pray Indian prayers, and sometimes we pray the Christian prayers we learned from Father Baraga in L'Anse. We pray to the Great Spirit to hear us and protect us. I prayed to him to bring Maria a friend, and he brought a white girl. He hears our prayers and surprises us."

Everybody smiled. They were thankful that an Indian girl and a white girl had become friends and that an Indian woman and a white woman were becoming friends. Now they all understood the prayer pictograph.

"I will draw one more," said Maria's mother, "but this one will take a whole sheet. There will be a group of twelve pictures."

Edith, Josette and Maria watched her draw twelve

boxes about an inch wide and two inches high. In the center of each box she drew something shaped like a crescent. "That looks like a banana," said Josette.

"I do not know 'banana,'" said Maria.

"A banana is a piece of yellow fruit shaped like a moon," said Josette.

Then Maria's mother drew a different picture above each "banana" until there were twelve different pictures, one for each of the boxes.

She wrote in English the name of the first box: Snow Moon.

"Oh," said Maria, "now I know. That is a moon. That's what a 'banana' is." The two girls laughed.

The next moon was Hunger Moon. Then followed Crow Moon, Grass Moon, Planting Moon, Rose Moon, Heat Moon, Thunder Moon, Hunting Moon, Falling Leaf Moon, Beaver Moon, and the twelfth was Long Night Moon.

"Now," said Maria's mother, "you girls fill in the English names under the moons."

"These are the months of the year," said Maria. "I know that January is the Snow Moon, and February is the Hunger Moon."

"Why is February the Hunger Moon?" asked Josette.

"That is the month when we starve if the snow is too deep and the hunting is bad," said Maria's mother. "We go to Father Baraga in L'Anse for food. Otherwise we die."

Josette and Maria printed in the rest of the months.

"We are now in the Thunder Moon," Josette observed, studying the drawings. "Will there be storms coming?"

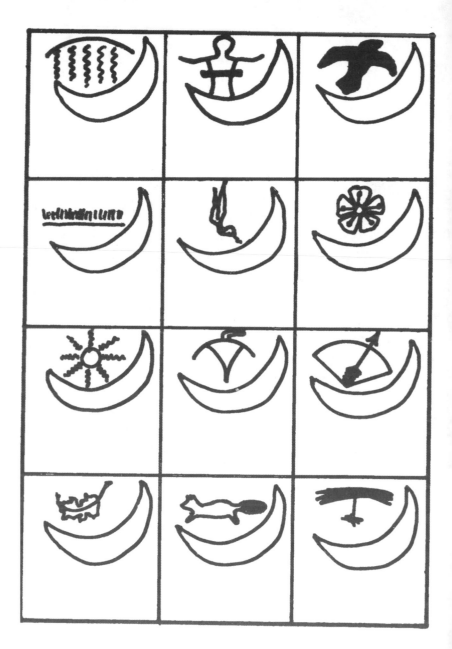

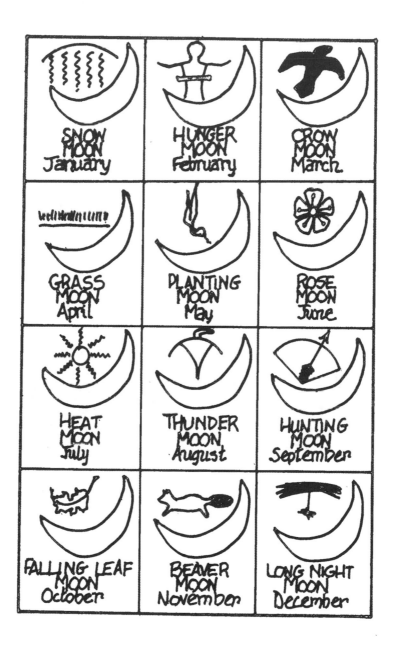

SNOW MOON January

HUNGER MOON February

CROW MOON March

GRASS MOON April

PLANTING MOON May

ROSE MOON June

HEAT MOON July

THUNDER MOON August

HUNTING MOON September

FALLING LEAF MOON October

BEAVER MOON November

LONG NIGHT MOON December

"Yes," said Maria's mother, "but sometimes the storms come in the Hunting Moon, too. You watch for ships that come to Copper Harbor in the Thunder Moon and in the Falling Moon. Storms may drown the ships. This Ojibwe calendar is for you. You keep it and remember us in the Hunger Moon month when we are far away. Now we must go."

"But Mr. Hayes and Edmund haven't come back yet," said Josette. "They wanted to meet you and find out about the scroll."

"We will try to get Maria's father to come to the fort to read the pictographs," said Maria's mother, "but Maria may come to see you every day. She can tell me about your baby," she added to Edith.

Edith thanked them for coming, and Josette walked with Maria and her mother to the entrance of the fort. She said hello to the soldier on guard and introduced Maria and her mother to him. "They will come often," she said to him, "but they are afraid. Will you always let them in?"

"Yes," said the soldier, "and I'll tell the other soldiers on guard to watch for them, too."

"Maria's father may come sometime, too," said Josette. "Will you let him in?"

"I'll have to check with Lieutenant Elliott on that," he said.

As Maria and her mother disappeared into the woods, Josette turned and saw the sheep being herded by Private Wilks and other soldiers with guns. Private Wilks said, "We're taking the sheep to a better pasture. There's no grass left here. If we want lamb roasts and lamb chops and warm wool in the fall and winter, we have to fatten them up."

Josette's favorite sheep, Mismatched, rubbed against her. "May I come with you?" Josette asked.

"If you have permission," Private Wilks said. "We don't want you getting lost again."

"But when I got lost," she said with a smile, "I found a friend, and her father can teach you how to build a canoe!"

Josette ran to the house, and Edith readily gave her permission. She knew Josette would be safe with Private Wilks.

Josette, the soldiers and the sheep walked for about a mile, the soldiers making sure that the sheep didn't drift off into the woods or try to swim away in the lake again. When they reached the grassy slopes, the soldiers herded the sheep into an enclosure they had already built there. The grass was thick and plentiful, and a brook ran through the enclosure. Josette petted Mismatched. Then she said, "Who's going to look after them?"

"Soldiers are being assigned to check up on them every day to make sure that they're getting enough water and grass." He paused. "And," he said, "we want to make sure that no wolves get in and kill them. If you'd like to check on your sheep, you may come with us. I'll let you know when we're coming to see them."

"Wolves?" said Josette. "Have you heard wolves around the fort?"

"Some soldiers say that they hear wolves howling at night, but we tell them that they're dreaming," said Private Wilks.

As they walked back to the fort, Josette thought about wolves. She remembered when she had heard wolves. That was when she had been in the Indian camp and was awakened by them in the night. But maybe she had been dreaming, too.

CHAPTER ELEVEN

woods

Edmund and Mr. Hayes were returning to the house when Josette came around the corner. "Did you find copper?" she called out to them.

"It looks promising," said Mr. Hayes. "So promising that I'll get a permit from the government agent to explore the site. The permit lasts for a year, and if the copper looks good I can get a lease to mine for three years. You may see me here for a long time."

"When are you going to start?" asked Josette. "I'd like to watch."

"In a couple weeks," Mr. Hayes answered. "My men are all busy now, but I hear the *John Jacob Astor* is coming in September with men looking for work. I can use some help in the mines."

As they entered the house, Josette remembered the scroll. "Maria's mother couldn't read the scroll," she said, "but Maria's father can—if we let him come into the fort."

"I'll leave the scroll here with you," Mr. Hayes said. "I know it's in good hands." He smiled at Josette.

"Maria's mother wrote Ojibwe pictures for us,"

Josette said. She showed Mr. Hayes and Edmund the pictographs. Edmund looked hard at the one with the man holding a gun.

"I don't like the looks of this one," Edmund said, "even though I'm not sure what it means."

"It's a man holding a gun," said Josette. "Maria's father says it's the white man at the fort holding a gun and that white men are here to kill Indians."

"I'm sorry to hear that he thinks that way about us," said Edmund. "We're not here to kill Indians—only to protect the miners."

"No Indians have bothered us," said Mr. Hayes. "In fact, we haven't even seen any Indians, except the fur traders passing through."

"May Maria's father come to the fort to read the scroll?" Josette asked Edmund.

Edmund hesitated. "I don't suppose there's any harm in talking to an Indian," he said. "After all, he did bring you back to us."

"Her father can read the scroll, and he can show Private Wilks how to build a birchbark canoe," said Josette.

Edmund put his arm around Josette. "You are a real peacemaker," he said. "No one could make friends with Indians as fast as you. And maybe we could *all* learn something from Maria's father."

As he was leaving, Mr. Hayes said that he hoped to see them again in a few weeks, if not before. He thanked them for telling him about the copper that the soldiers had discovered. "The first small nugget of copper that we find goes to you, Josette," he said.

That night in bed Josette was awakened by bright moonlight shining into her window. She got up and looked out. The moon made a silver path on the lake and in her room. It almost seemed she should be able to walk on the path, it was so bright. In the moonlight, the trees on the other side of the lake had silver arms reaching out to her from across the water. She wondered where Gullie was sleeping, and she thought about how white the sheep would look in their new enclosure with the moon shining on their wool.

She wasn't sleepy and stood at the window for a few minutes more. Before turning to crawl back into bed, she thought she saw something moving in the woods. She remembered the bear that had come to fish in the lake her first day at Fort Wilkins, and she stood very still, watching for the mother bear and her two cubs. The leaves on the saplings seemed to be trembling as something moved through them. She waited. Then something gray pushed its way through the trees and stood on the shore of the lake. She could see that it was not a bear—it wasn't big enough and it wasn't the right color. She looked harder as it moved closer to the lake. The moonlight shone on it, making it gloriously bright.

It hesitated, standing still for a few minutes and sniffing the air. Then it put its head up in the air and howled. Now she knew what it was. It was a wolf! It had come to drink from the lake. After it finished drinking, the wolf plunged into the water and swam across to her side of the lake, not far from her house. It stopped to rest below her window. Josette half-hoped that it wouldn't look up and see her. She could hardly breathe.

Josette wondered what a wolf was doing on the grounds of the fort. She watched as it trotted past the two canoes on the shore and past the building where the soldiers were sleeping. It headed for the sheep enclosure, looked around, seemed puzzled, sniffed, then howled again, putting its head in the air. Finding the enclosure empty and the sheep gone, the wolf howled again and again. Then it disappeared into the deep woods along Lake Superior, and Josette could no longer see it.

Josette wondered what the wolf would find to eat in the woods on Lake Superior—a mink, an otter, a wolverine? She wondered if the soldiers had been awakened by the wolf's howling.

The next morning Josette couldn't wait to tell Edith and Edmund what she had seen in the moonlight. "Why didn't you call me?" said Edmund. "I could have shot him."

"He didn't hurt me," said Josette. "He didn't even see me."

"But I don't like a wolf hanging around the fort and under your window," said Edith. "Who knows what he would attack. He's obviously looking for food."

"I wonder if the soldiers on guard saw it," said Edmund. "I'll ask them when we go out for drill. Wolves may be more of a danger here than Indians."

After breakfast Josette helped Edith clean the house, and then she did her reading and arithmetic and practiced the piano. But she couldn't stop thinking about the wolf. She wondered where he lived and how many other wolves lived with him. She made up a little melody at the piano. She called it her wolf song.

In midafternoon Private Wilks stopped by and told Josette and Edith that he and Private Hawkins were going to check on the sheep. He asked Josette if she'd like to come along.

Josette said yes, and Edith agreed to let her go.

They followed the path to Copper Harbor, and then they left the track and walked through the woods. The woods were not as thick here. In the open spaces they saw low-growing bushes with bright blue berries on them. Private Wilks identified them as blueberries. He showed Josette the difference between blueberries and the beadlily berries that were bright blue and growing next to the blueberries. The beadlily berries were bigger and iridescent blue, and, he stressed, they were poisonous. "Never eat one of these, not even one," he said.

Josette looked closely at the two kinds of berries. Then she and the two soldiers picked a handful of blueberries and ate them. They were very sweet and juicy. "Maybe I could come here and pick some for Edith," Josette suggested. "And maybe the bakers would like them to make blueberry muffins."

"Don't come here alone," said Private Wilks. "If you want blueberries, ask me after supper to go with you. You know what happened the last time you were out picking berries."

"I won't go alone," said Josette, "but if I tell Maria, she can come with me. She knows her way through the woods."

By this time they were nearing the sheep enclosure. Although they couldn't see it yet, they could hear the sheep baa-aa-ing. "Something's disturbing them," said Private Wilks. "They never made that much noise at the fort."

Josette ran ahead of Private Wilks and Private Hawkins, hoping that Mismatched would come up to the fence and recognize her. The sheep were huddled together, not grazing peacefully on the lush grass or drinking water from the bubbling brook. They were pushing against the fence so hard they were bending it.

Private Wilks and Private Hawkins hopped over the fence and jumped into the enclosure. "Don't come in here, Josette," they called to her. They had already seen streaks of bright red on the ground and in the grass, and as they got closer they knew it was blood. They saw white wool soaked in red blood.

Josette looked past the fence and saw the streaks of bright red on the ground and in the grass. "What is that?" she called to them.

Then she saw that the red had saturated something. That something was wool.

Private Wilks and Private Hawkins couldn't shield her from the sight. There was blood all over the wool. Someone had slit the animals' throats and torn away their flesh. The legs of one sheep had been torn off. Private Wilks tried to stand in front of the sheep with the legs torn off so that Josette wouldn't see it. That sheep had mismatched ears. "Three sheep have been killed," said Private Hawkins.

Josette looked away. "Who did this?" she asked, too stunned to cry.

Private Wilks and Private Hawkins examined the grass. "These are wolf prints," said Private Hawkins.

"No doubt about it," said Private Wilks. "They're hungry, and the sheep are easy prey."

"I told my bunkmates at the fort this morning at breakfast that I heard wolves during the night, but no one believed me," said Private Hawkins.

"I believe you," said Josette. "I saw a wolf last night from my bedroom window."

"On the fort grounds?" the soldiers asked.

"I saw it under my window. Then it went past your quarters and over to the old sheep enclosure," said Josette.

"These wolves had a feast, said Private Wilks.

Josette said, "I wonder where Mismatched is. They're all huddled together so I can't see her."

Private Wilks and Private Hawkins picked up the dead sheep. "We'll take the carcasses back to the fort," Private Wilks said. "Maybe we can do something with the wool."

"It's better for the sheep here not to have the dead ones around," said Private Hawkins. "Now they can get back to grazing without being afraid that wolves will attack them."

"May I look for Mismatched before we go?" asked Josette. "I can recognize her by her ears."

"Go ahead," said Private Wilks. "But be careful. They're guarding themselves from predators. They may not like you pushing your way into their flock."

Private Wilks helped Josette over the fence. She tried hard to find Mismatched, but the sheep didn't want to let her separate them. They stuck close, baa-aa-ing together, trying to shield each other from attackers. Even though there were only seventeen sheep left, she couldn't find her sheep with the mismatched ears.

While she was searching on the edges of the flock, Private Wilks and Private Hawkins examined the sheep carcasses. Private Wilks said, "Let's not tell Josette. I'll carry it so she can't see the ears."

On the way back to the fort, Josette asked Private Wilks, "What if wolves come again tonight?"

"We'll ask Lieutenant Elliott to send men to guard the sheep at night until fall. Then our cooks will butcher them so we'll have meat in the cold winter months," said Private Hawkins.

Josette was quiet for the rest of the walk. She was so worried about Mismatched that she didn't think to look at what was left of the poor dead sheep that Private Wilks and Private Hawkins were carrying. She remembered the beautiful wolf that she saw shining in the moonlight.

She hoped he was not one of the killers.

CHAPTER TWELVE

treaty

It was now September, and the days were warm and golden. Gullie woke up earlier and earlier every morning. It was barely light when Josette heard his ""Hiyah . . . hiyah . . . hiyah . . . yuk-yuckle-yuckle." He seemed to sense that September in the North was the far edge of winter and that, when the snow came, he would have to leave for warmer places. If he stayed at Fort Wilkins, his food supply of fish would be hidden under the frozen surfaces of the lakes and streams, and then his song would be frozen, too.

The second week in September Edmund announced at breakfast that he and Dr. Isaacs were going to make a canoe trip to L'Anse before the autumn storms hit the lake, making travel impossible. Edmund had heard horror stories from John Hayes about how fierce the storms were and how cold and desolate winter was here and how short the days. Night comes as early as three o'clock in the afternoon. Hayes had said, "Not everybody can survive six months of frozen white."

"Captain Clary is sending me down to Father Baraga in L'Anse to see if he can come here for Christmas," Edmund explained. "The soldiers are far away from home and will be missing their families. Some haven't seen their own wives and children since May, and they might feel especially sad at Christmas. We want to make Christmas a happy time for them." He added, "Also, Dr. Isaacs needs to check on the health of the Indian settlement. We're canoeing to the bottom of the Keweenaw Peninsula."

"How long will you be gone?" Edith asked. "You know I'm getting close to my time."

"About a week," Edmund answered. "We have to go now while the bay is still calm. We can't wait much longer because storms may come at the end of the month, and then it will be too dangerous."

"Just the two of you?" worried Edith. "You don't know the way, and you haven't paddled many canoes."

"We've studied the maps," he said reassuringly. "We think we've chosen the shortest way." He went on, "We'll go north to Keweenaw Point and reach the bay up there. Once we're on the bay, we can canoe along the shore where we'll be protected from the strong westerly wind all the way down to L'Anse. I don't know anybody who's familiar with the bay, but maybe we should ask Private Wilks to come with us. At least he's a good paddler."

"Why don't you ask Maria's father?" Josette suggested.

"Do you think he would come?" Edmund asked. He hesitated to tell Josette that he didn't like to ask an Indian to guide them to Father Baraga's mission. What if Maria's father took them captive, or worse yet, killed them? After all, the Indians thought of the soldiers as enemies, and Edmund was an important commissioned officer.

"Maria's coming to see me today," said Josette. "We can ask her to ask her father."

Edmund thought about Josette's idea. He had to admit to himself that he didn't look forward to the trip, although he hadn't said so to Edith and Josette. There were so many unpredictable hazards for three men who had no experience in canoeing the waters of the bay.

"I'd feel a lot better if Maria's father guided you," said Edith.

Just then there was a light tap on the door. It was Maria.

Josette immediately told her about Edmund's plans. Edmund said, "Do you think your father would take Dr. Isaacs and me to L'Anse to see Father Baraga? I would pay him."

"I'll ask him," said Maria. "Do you want to go soon? In a few weeks it is the Falling Leaf Moon. Then we go duck hunting. The next month is the Beaver Moon, when we hunt for bear and wolf and deer and fox and beaver. We are gone away hunting for a long time."

"Then it will have to be soon. We'll leave tomorrow, if the weather stays good," said Edmund, "and if your father is willing."

"May we go right now to ask him?" asked Josette.

"What do you mean by 'we?'" Edith asked.

"May Josette come with me? Josette can talk to my father. He likes her. I will bring her back to you." Maria spoke politely and reasonably.

Edith and Edmund exchanged glances, then Edith nodded "yes," and Edmund agreed, but Edith said the girls could not leave until Maria helped them finish eating breakfast. Edith quickly gave Maria a cup of tea and a piece of toast with strawberry jam.

After breakfast, Maria and Josette left for the Indian

camp, promising to be back before dark with the answer from Maria's father. Josette was happy all the way to the camp. She followed Maria, just as she had done when Maria rescued her from the bears. She noticed that the trees were turning red and gold and bronze. In some places the leaves had already fallen, and she noticed their crisp, crunchy sound under her feet.

Soon they arrived at the Indian camp. Maria's mother was surprised to see Josette, and Maria's father approached the girls immediately. He did not seem unfriendly to Josette, but he asked Maria why she was back so soon and why she had brought Josette into their camp again. Maria let Josette answer her father.

Josette looked up into his eyes and said, "I have a message for you. Edmund, my brother-in-law, is going to L'Anse to see Father Baraga, and Dr. Isaacs is going with him to check on the health of the Indians there. Edmund and Dr. Isaacs don't know anything about canoeing or about the bay. Will you go with them and guide them in a canoe?"

There. She had said it without flinching. She saw a small smile in the corner of Maria's father's mouth. "You are a charming little girl," he said. "Who could say 'no' to you? When do they want to go?"

"Tomorrow," said Maria.

"Edmund will pay you," added Josette.

"I do not need pay," said Maria's father. "Father Baraga is good to us in the Hunger Moon. He gives us food when we are starving. He has taught us English. I will go for his sake."

"When will you come to the fort?"

"Early tomorrow morning," he replied, "before the sun rises. You tell your brother-in-law to be ready. I will come in my canoe on Lake Superior across from the fort. They will travel with me."

"Let's hurry back and tell him," said Josette.

"No hurry," said Maria's mother. "First you rest and eat. Then you go."

Josette suddenly thought of something. "May Maria stay overnight with me? Then she won't have to walk all the way back tonight."

Maria's mother and father exchanged glances. Maria's mother nodded approval, and Maria's father agreed. Josette and Maria smiled at each other. Real friends like to stay overnight and talk from their beds in the dark. They can tell each other secrets in the dark that they would never tell in the light. The girls were happy with the plan.

After they had rested and eaten, they began their trip back with the good news that Maria's father would guide Edmund and Dr. Isaacs to L'Anse. Josette knew that Edith would be relieved. She would trust Maria's father, even though she had never met him.

When they arrived back at the fort, just before dark, Edmund was waiting for them at the entrance. He and Edith had been getting a little worried. When he saw Josette and Maria coming out of the woods, he waved at them and called out, "Do you have good news for me?"

"Yes," they both answered. Then Maria continued, "You must be ready to leave early in the morning, before sunrise, and my father will take you to L'Anse."

Edith sighed with relief. Then she said that it was almost dark and that Maria couldn't make another trip back to her camp because it was so late.

"I know that," said Josette, "so I asked her to stay overnight. She can sleep in my room. Her mother said she could stay."

"In that case let's have a little supper," said Edith, "and celebrate."

After supper Edmund brought up a cot from the soldiers' quarters and carried it into Josette's room. The girls went to bed early because they were so tired, but they didn't fall asleep immediately. They talked about themselves. Maria said that she was glad she was an Indian but that sometimes she worried that there wasn't room any more for Indians. She didn't know where they'd go if miners took over all the land. She wondered if there was room in Virginia for them, where Josette came from. Josette confided in Maria that she wondered how long they would be up north, and if they didn't stay long, whether she would ever see Maria again. Maybe there was room in Virginia for them. She'd ask Edith. Then they grew drowsy and fell asleep.

The next thing they knew it was morning. Josette woke up first. "Listen," she said to Maria, who was just beginning to wake up. It was Gullie on the roof. He was singing his only song, "Hiyah . . . hiyah . . . hiyah . . . yuk-yuckle-yuckle." The girls could also hear Edmund and Edith whispering over their breakfast in the kitchen. They dressed quickly, and by the time they got downstairs they heard Maria's father tapping on the door.

Josette and Maria joined Edmund and Edith, and they walked with Maria's father on the path to Lake Superior. They loaded the canoe while Maria's father explained to them the route they were taking. "We do not go the shortest way," he said. "We avoid Keweenaw Point. The water there is too stormy. Do you know what *Keweenaw* means?"

"No," said Edmund.

"It is the Ojibwe word that means *place-where-we-*

make-short-cut-on foot. We canoe on Lake Superior first. Then we carry our canoe across the land into Portage Lake. That is where we go on the bay. Then we land at L'Anse."

"Oh, I am so glad you are guiding them," said Edith to Maria's father. "They were going to canoe over Keweenaw Point because it is shorter and so they wouldn't have to portage the canoe."

"They would have drowned," said Maria's father.

The moment that followed was very quiet. Then Dr. Isaacs appeared carrying his medical bag. "I'm ready," he said, introducing himself to Maria's father. "I want to meet Father Baraga. He's a famous priest here in the North country."

"He is a wonderful man," said Maria's father. "He feeds us when we are hungry. He teaches us English. He is writing down our Ojibwe language. Then we will be able to read our own language."

When everything was carefully packed, they said goodbye. "God go with you," said Edith.

"He goes with us always," said Maria's father.

Edith, Josette, and Maria watched them go. Maria's father guided his canoe out of the little cove, and then they were gone.

On the way back to the house, Edith said, "Ouch."

"Is something the matter?" said Josette. "Did you stub your toe on a rock?"

"No," said Edith. "I had a pain that makes me think the baby will be coming. It may be my first labor pain."

They reached the house, and Edith sat down.

"Are you feeling more pains?" Josette asked anxiously.

"Not right now," said Edith.

"Shall I get my mother?" Maria suggested. "She can help you. She will know if the baby is coming."

Josette thought about Edith and the baby. She didn't want to be alone with Edith if the baby was coming, and Dr. Isaacs was on his way to L'Anse with Edmund. "May Maria get her mother, just in case the baby is coming?" she asked.

Edith hesitated. She didn't want Maria's mother to walk all the way from the camp if this was a false alarm. She knew that sometimes labor pains started and then stopped. The baby wasn't due for about two weeks. But she thought too of how comforting it would be to have Maria's mother here, just in case the baby came today. Before she could consent, Maria said, "I will get my mother. She has delivered many babies."

"Take something to eat with you," said Edith, handing her a slice of bread, a piece of cheese and an apple.

"I will run," said Maria.

Edith went to lie down while Josette made herself breakfast. Though Edith had eaten with Edmund, she welcomed a cup of tea. She didn't tell Josette that she was feeling a few more labor pains. She hoped Maria's mother would arrive in time.

Several hours passed while they waited, and Edith and Josette cleaned the house. Edith wanted to keep active, hoping that working would help to ease the pain. Again she showed Josette the cradle that they had brought from Virginia. She explained that this cradle had been in their family for generations and that Josette was the last baby to sleep in it. The new baby would sleep in a cradle that had rocked babies for many years.

After they had cleaned every surface that Edith could find, she said, "Now I think we're ready. Will you put on a big kettle of water over the fire so that it will be boiling when Maria's mother comes? I'm feeling the pains regularly now."

Josette went out with a bucket and filled it with water from the lake. As she looked up, she saw Maria and her mother at the entrance to the fort. She waved and waited for them eagerly.

"Good," said Maria's mother when she saw the bucket. "We will need boiling water and soap. We will need at least two buckets of water."

Maria's mother was carrying a bag made of mink skin. She explained to Josette that this was a Midewiwin bag that an Ojibwe medicine woman kept for her whole life. She showed Josette what was in her bag. She held up herb medicines, the skull of an animal, a stone bowl, and a mullein spike. "After an Ojibwe medicine woman dies or is too old to practice medicine, the bag goes to her daughter. This will be Maria's medicine bag when I am gone," she said.

When they entered the house, Edith said, "I'm so glad you're here. The pains are coming faster now." Josette and Maria poured the water into the big kettle and got another bucketful. Before they hung the kettle, they put another log on the fire to make sure the water would boil quickly.

Maria's mother said to Edith, "First I will light a mullein candle." After lighting the spike, she chanted a prayer. Edith said "Amen" when Maria's mother had finished the chant.

The mullein candle burned evenly and made the room smell good. Josette remembered the pictograph for prayer—the sky and a mullein candle burning. Josette said to Maria's mother, "May we stay to help and watch?"

Maria's mother asked Edith if the girls could stay. "Yes," said Edith, bent over in pain.

Maria's mother made Edith comfortable on the couch. She told her to breathe in and out when the pains came. She washed her hands in hot water and soap. Then she examined Edith. "It's coming," she said. Edith tried not to scream. The pain was intense.

"Drink this," said Maria's mother, and Edith swallowed a spoonful of strange-tasting liquid. "It will help you." Maria's mother did not tell Edith that this medicine was the blood of a garter snake's head mixed with water, used to help a mother in childbirth. Edith didn't ask any questions.

"I see the baby's head," said Maria's mother after a while. "Now, push. Push. Push!"

Josette and Maria could not believe what was happening. They saw the baby's head slide out. Then, after Edith pushed again, they saw a shoulder. Maria's mother helped the other shoulder to slide out. Then the whole baby was there.

Maria's mother patted the baby until it cried. "It's a boy," she said. She laid the baby on Edith's stomach, and Edith stroked him and slid him up to her breasts and kissed him. Then she examined him carefully to see if he had ten fingers and ten toes, and she cried for joy. She said over and over to Maria's mother, "Thank you for coming!" Maria's mother washed Edith while Edith stroked her newborn son.

Then Maria's mother took the baby from Edith and bathed him in a pan of warm water to wash off the birth fluids. His hair was plastered on his head, and Maria's mother washed his hair very gently, showing the girls how to wash and rinse it. After the hair was washed, it turned out to be reddish blonde, like Edith's and Josette's.

Josette brought the baby clothes to Maria's mother, who pinned the diaper on and slipped the baby into a little flannel gown that Edith had made for him. Then she wrapped him in the baby quilt that Edith had been wrapped in when she was a baby, and she laid him in the crib next to Edith's couch.

"Now we take care of the baby's mother," she said to Edith. "You must drink some wintergreen tea before you go to sleep."

Josette got the teapot down from the shelf, and Maria's mother put in a few dried wintergreen leaves that she took out of her bag and poured boiling water over the leaves. When the tea had steeped, she poured it into a cup and then added honey. The room smelled like the woods, pungent and spicy.

Edith listened for breathing sounds from her baby while she waited for the tea. Fast asleep in his cradle next to the couch, the baby was breathing so softly she could hardly hear him. The wintergreen tea made her feel drowsy, and as she drank, she drifted off to sleep. Maria's mother had to rescue the cup from her hand.

Josette and Maria looked at the sleeping baby in the cradle. A shaft of sunlight shone on the cradle and on his red gold hair.

CHAPTER THIRTEEN

woman

Josette and Maria slept so soundly that night that they didn't even hear the baby cry when he was hungry. They didn't hear Maria's mother in the kitchen the next morning until she called them for breakfast. When they came down, Edith was eating breakfast in bed. She was saying to Maria's mother that she'd like to get up and eat breakfast with them at the table. "You must stay in bed today, and maybe tomorrow you get up," said Maria's mother. "We make sure that you are strong enough."

The first thing that Josette said to Maria's mother at breakfast was, "Will you stay with us until Edmund gets back?"

"Yes," said Maria's mother. "I cannot leave Edith alone with you and the baby. But I will go back to the camp to get some things. We must make a dreamcatcher to hang over his cradle."

"What is a dreamcatcher?" said Josette.

"I will tell you when I get back from camp. Then you and Maria can help me make one. The baby must have a dreamcatcher before the next night."

Before Maria's mother left she bathed Edith and the baby while Josette and Maria did the dishes, made the beds, and cleaned up the house. Edith and the baby soon fell asleep. Josette and Maria brought in fresh water from the lake and some wood for the fires. Then Josette said to Maria, "I must tell Captain Clary that the baby is here." Maria stayed with Edith and the baby while Josette went to see Captain Clary.

He was surprised at the news of the baby's arrival but said, "We'll celebrate when Lieutenant Elliott gets back from L'Anse." Then he paused, looked intently at Josette and said, "Dr. Isaacs was gone. Who delivered the baby? Not you?"

"No," said Josette, "Maria's mother."

"Who's Maria?" the Captain asked. "I don't know any Maria. There's no Maria or her mother at the fort."

"They're Indians, Ojibwe," said Josette. "Maria's father is taking Edmund to L'Anse."

"I know about the Indian guide who's taking Lieutenant Elliott and Dr. Isaacs to L'Anse, but I didn't know about an Indian girl who comes to the fort to visit you," said Captain Clary. "Is her mother here now?"

"Yes," said Josette. "I am friends with Maria. She rescued me from a bear. Maria's mother has delivered many babies. She helped Edith. She's going to stay with us until Edmund gets back."

Captain Clary smiled. "Maybe we aren't needed up here if Indians have friends like you," he said.

As she walked back, she met Private Wilks and told him about the baby. "May I see him?" he said and joined her to return to the house.

Maria was waiting for Josette. When she saw Private Wilks, she wondered if something was wrong and if she'd have to leave the fort, but Private Wilks was very friendly. By this time Edith was awake.

"Welcome," she said to Private Wilks, "and look at my beautiful son."

The baby was also waking up and blinking at the world with big blue eyes. Private Wilks didn't know what to say, so he said, "He's so tiny. He's the smallest soldier at the fort. We'll have to fly a little flag over his cradle."

Just then the baby began to cry and Private Wilks said he had to be going. Edith asked Josette to hand the baby to her so she could nurse him.

Not long after, Maria's mother returned. She was still carrying her Midewiwin bag, but she also had another bag. "Now I will tell you about the dreamcatcher," she said.

She took out of the bag short branches from a willow tree, long strands of animal sinew, colored feathers, and shiny beads. "The dreamcatcher catches bad dreams," she said. "We make a hole in the middle of the dreamcatcher so that good dreams go through the hole. The bad dreams get caught in the web we make. It is like a spider web that catches flies. It catches all the bad dreams, so the baby will have only good dreams. Then the baby smiles in his sleep."

Josette and Maria sat next to Maria's mother and watched her. First she took a willow branch and shaped it into a small circle. Then she tied the ends of the circle together with a piece of animal sinew. "This sinew comes from a deer," she said. "Sinew is the tissue that connects his muscles to his bones."

"When did you catch the deer?" asked Josette.

"In the fall, before he was hungry and lean, when he still had a lot of fat on him. We save his meat for winter when we are hungry and cold. We need meat for food and deerskin to keep warm. Maria's father shot him with an arrow. He was a good deer, full of sweet meat and healthy skin. After we cleaned him and cut off his coat, we took the sinew because it is strong and will not break. We turn the sinew into thread by pulling it through our teeth and softening it into strands like thread. We use it to sew blankets and coats and dreamcatchers. But we always remember the deer who gave us his meat and his coat."

She took the sinew and began to weave it into loops inside the willow ring. She made a web pattern of loops in the hoop. It took as long as it takes a spider to weave a web. While she was weaving the web, she told them a story.

"A long time ago a spider was spinning a web near the bed of a grandmother named Nokomis. Every day the grandmother watched the spider spin its web. Then one day her grandson came in to visit his grandmother. He saw the spider hanging over her bed, and he lifted his moccasin to kill it. Quickly his grandmother held his arm back and said, 'No, my dear grandson, do not harm the spider. The spider makes a web so that it can live.' The grandson was puzzled. After he left, the spider talked to the grandmother and thanked her for saving its life. The spider said, 'I offer a gift to you in exchange for my life. Watch me tonight as I weave my web. Then you will learn how to make a web. In your web you can capture the bad dreams and the nightmares that want to attack you when you sleep. But you must remember to make a hole in the center as I do in my web. The good dreams will find the opening in the web. The good dreams come from the Good Spirit and will enter your heart all the days of your life. You must hang the dreamcatcher over your bed.' The grandmother made a dreamcatcher to hang over her own bed. She made it out of willow and sinew and feathers and beads. Then she taught the other women in her tribe to make dreamcatchers. Everybody slept under a dreamcatcher. The dream spirits gave good sleep to everybody in the tribe. No evil dreams, we call them *bawedjigewin*, ever molested them again."

When Maria's mother was finished weaving the web, Maria said, "It looks just like a spider web, only there aren't any flies in it."

"But can you find the hole?" Maria's mother asked them. The web was so intricately woven that at first they missed the hole. Maria's mother handed the dreamcatcher to Josette. "Oh, I see it; it's here." Josette pointed to it and ran her finger around it.

"Do you think a good dream can find the hole?" Maria's mother asked them.

"I don't know," said Maria. Maria's mother handed each of them a beautiful feather. One was bright blue from a blue jay, the other bright red from a cardinal.

"Shall we tie our feathers to it so the good dream can find it?" said Maria.

"Yes," said Maria's mother, smiling. "Tie a string of sinew on the tip of each feather, and then tie the two feathers to the top and bottom of the hole."

Josette tied her bright blue jay feather to the top of the hole, and Maria tied her bright red cardinal feather to the bottom of the hole. "The good dreams will find it and slip through," said Josette, "and the bad dreams will be scared of it."

"The feathers remind us of the air that we breathe. The baby will breathe in pure air when he sees the feathers, and he will be healthy," Maria's mother said.

"Is the dreamcatcher finished?" asked Maria.

"Not yet," said Maria's mother. "Take another piece of sinew and tie it on these feathers." This time she gave

Maria a feather from an eagle and Josette a feather from an owl. "The baby needs the eagle feather for courage and the owl feather for wisdom," she explained.

They tied a piece of sinew on the top of each feather. "Now tie the feathers to the bottom of the dreamcatcher.

Leave a long enough piece of sinew on each one so that it will float on the breeze. Then the baby can see it when he is in his cradle."

They hung the eagle feather and the owl feather side by side on the bottom of the dreamcatcher. "It's beautiful," said Josette, blowing on the hanging feathers.

"Would you like to add a bead?" Maria's mother said to them. "You can string a bead and then attach it anywhere."

Josette took a bright purple bead and attached it near the top of the dreamcatcher. Maria took a pink bead and attached it just opposite to Josette's. "Now it is finished," said Maria's mother.

The baby was just waking up. Maria's mother picked him up, changed him and took him to his mother. The girls showed Edith the dreamcatcher that they had made for the baby. Then they attached it to the cradle. It hung where the baby could see it, swaying a little in the gentle breeze that floated in from the open window.

Josette thought that there was nothing better than having a friend like Maria, a friend's mother like Maria's mother, a sister like Edith, and a new baby in the house. Living in the North on Lake Superior far from Virginia was the best place in the world to be. And soon Edmund would be back. When he had left there was an empty cradle, and Edith had trouble seeing her feet. When he returned, there would be someone in the cradle. And there would be a dreamcatcher to catch all the bad dreams in its web. The good dreams would pass through the beautiful hole with the blue and red feathers showing the way. Every night the good dreams would come back and enter the baby's head and heart. He would dream beautiful dreams.

CHAPTER FOURTEEN

talk

The week passed by quickly. In two days Edith could get up and eat breakfast at the table and could bathe herself and the baby. In three days she could walk to the bakery and get fresh bread each morning. It was still so warm outdoors in the afternoon that Edith sat with the baby on the porch where the baby could breathe in the pure air of the lake and the woods. Many of the soldiers stopped to see Lieutenant Elliot's son and to wish him a happy life. When the soldiers came, Maria's mother hid indoors. She was still afraid of the soldiers, but she let Maria go outside with Edith, Josette and the baby.

The fourth day, Maria's mother asked Maria and Josette to pick berries. "Now the blueberries and bilberries and blackberries are ripe," she said. Edith longed for fresh fruit, and she didn't worry about Josette if she was with Maria. The girls each picked up a basket for gathering the berries. "Put the bilberries and the blackberries on the bottom," Edith said, "they are the heavy berries, and put the little blueberries on the top."

Maria led the way through the woods to where the berries grew. Josette had never seen such big berries. The bilberries were so plump and juicy that they sometimes burst in the hands when picked. The girls laid them gently on the bottom of their baskets but couldn't help eating a few. The blackberries were big and bumpy. It was easy to fill half the baskets with bilberries and blackberries. Josette and Maria ate blackberries until their tongues and fingers and teeth were stained bright purple. They had to look in a different place to find blueberries, and the blueberries took much longer to pick because they were so small, but finally the baskets were filled.

When the girls brought their overflowing baskets home, Edith said that she had never seen bilberries before and that the blackberries were bigger than those she had picked in Virginia as a girl. Then she suggested, "Wouldn't the berries be delicious if we poured thick cream over them?"

"I'll go to the sutler's store," Josette offered, "and see if he has any cream."

"Maybe he'd like some blueberries, we have so many," said Edith.

Josette poured some of the blueberries into a small basket, and she and Maria took them to the sutler.

"I haven't eaten blueberries since I came up here," he said. "I'll take them to the bakers' and see if they'll make me a few blueberry muffins."

"We're wondering if you have fresh cream today," said Josette. "We have so many berries, Edith would like to eat them with cream."

"How did you guess?" said the sutler. "The fresh cream came this morning." He poured some thick cream into a jar for Josette and Maria.

"Here is money for them," said Josette. She held out some coins to him.

"I can't take money for the cream," he said, "not

after you brought me such beautiful blueberries. This is a present for Edith. When she is well enough to walk here, I have a gift for the new baby, too."

The fifth day, late in the afternoon, Maria's mother took out a small net from her pack and showed Josette and Maria how to put it in the lake to catch fish. "Edith needs fresh meat," said Maria's mother. "It will make her strong." While they lowered the net, Gullie watched them, first from the top of the roof, then from right next to Josette on the bank.

"We must be patient," said Maria's mother. "We must not pull up the net before it is time. We must not scare the fish or we will have no fish at all."

They waited for what seemed a long time. Although they were close to the canoes, Josette did not suggest that they go fishing in the canoe, even though she had seen Private Wilks and Private Hawkins fishing with poles from the canoe. She wondered whether fishing with a pole was faster than net fishing.

But Maria's mother was patient. She tested the net by tugging on it gently to see if it felt heavy. When it was heavy enough, she pulled up the net. There were four trout swimming in it. "Just enough for supper," she said.

The sixth day, the day before Edmund and Maria's father were expected back, Josette was getting anxious for Edmund to come home. She missed him, and she hoped that nothing had happened to him. Edith was up most of the day now, and she and Maria's mother talked a lot, mostly about the baby. Josette began to get restless and told Edith that she'd like to go to the sheep enclosure and see Mismatched. She had neglected Mismatched in all the excitement about the baby.

Edith said that if Josette was worried about

Mismatched, she should ask Private Wilks if he would take her and Maria to the sheep enclosure. When they came to Private Wilks, he hesitated. "Are you too busy right now?" Josette asked, sensing his hesitation.

"No, I'm not too busy," he said, "but are you sure that you want to take the long walk to the enclosure?" He didn't want to tell Josette that Mismatched had been killed by wolves. "You don't have to worry about the sheep," he said. "They're fine now. They're guarded every night by soldiers."

"But I'd like to see Mismatched," Josette said, "and I'd like Maria to see Mismatched, too."

Private Wilks didn't know how to avoid the subject any longer so he agreed to take them late that afternoon. Josette and Maria enjoyed the walk with Private Wilks. He and Maria exchanged knowledge about the plants and the trees. They stopped at the blueberry patch and ate berries by the handful. Private Wilks was in no hurry to get to the sheep enclosure, but at last they were there.

"There are many sheep," said Maria.

"Let's count them," said Josette, "and let's look for Mismatched."

They scrambled over the fence and entered the grassy enclosure. The sheep were grazing safely. They looked content and didn't even look up when Josette and Maria climbed into the enclosure. Maria began to count sheep while Josette wandered through the flock looking for Mismatched.

"Sixteen. Seventeen," Maria counted out loud. All were accounted for. But Josette still hadn't found a sheep with mismatched ears, and Maria hadn't seen one, either. No sheep came to Josette, looked into her eyes, and rubbed against her.

"Mismatched! Mismatched!" she called, but no sheep responded to her voice. "I can't find Mismatched," she said to Private Wilks. Her voice was trembling.

Private Wilks had to tell her the truth. "Josette, Mismatched died the night the wolves attacked the sheep."

Josette's eyes filled with tears. "Did a wolf eat her?" she asked.

"Yes," said Private Wilks. "I didn't want to tell you." He paused. "We even have her mismatched ears to identify her. We saved her wool. Maybe Maria's mother can wash the wool and make it into a blanket for the baby. It will keep him warm when winter comes."

"Then I can remember her," said Josette. "And I still have Gullie. I hope he doesn't leave in the winter. I hope he doesn't get eaten by an eagle."

"Don't worry," said Private Wilks. "Gullie's smart enough to hide from eagles. Maybe before winter comes, he'll fly south, and when he comes back in the spring he'll have white wings and a gold beak."

"Do you think he'll remember to come back?" Josette said to Private Wilks.

"I'm sure of it," he said. "Gullie seems to find you wherever he goes."

The seventh morning after the baby's birth, when the women and girls were eating breakfast, the door opened, and there stood Edmund and Maria's father. Edith jumped up from the breakfast table and threw her arms around her husband. He gathered her up in his arms, and he suddenly saw that she was thin. "What happened?" he said, before looking at the cradle.

"Look," said Edith pointing to the cradle. Then she stopped. "But I have not welcomed Maria's father." She greeted him and invited him to stay for breakfast and to tell them all about their trip. Then she turned to Edmund, who was staring into the cradle.

"What is it?" he said in amazement.

"A baby," laughed Edith.

"I can see that," said Edmund, "but what kind?"

"He's a boy," said Edith.

"When did he come?" Edmund said.

"The same day you left," said Edith.

"A boy. A boy," he said over and over again. "The day I left."

"Don't you want to know who delivered the baby?" asked Edith.

"Oh," said Edmund, "not Josette. It couldn't be Josette. And Dr. Isaacs was with me."

"Maria's mother," said Edith. "You know her. She is here standing behind you with her husband and Maria."

"Thank you, thank you," said Edmund to Maria's mother. "I cannot repay you for helping Edith."

Maria's mother replied, "No thanks. We must go now."

"No, no, you must stay. Maria's father must have breakfast with us," said Edmund. "Without Maria's father we would have drowned on the way back from L'Anse. Even on the way *to* L'Anse if we had gone over Keweenaw Point. We owe our lives to him, and we owe our baby to you," he said to Maria's mother. "Please stay and eat with us."

It was a joyful breakfast. Everyone talked at once. Josette tried to tell Edmund how Maria's mother had delivered the baby, and Edmund tried to tell them about the storm that had struck them on the way back from L'Anse and that if Maria's father hadn't been with them they would now be resting on the bottom of Lake Superior.

Edith finally remembered that they had gone to L'Anse to invite Father Baraga to come for Christmas. She asked Edmund, "Is Father Baraga coming for Christmas and," she added, "to baptize our baby?"

"Yes," said Edmund, "even if it's snowing hard, he'll come on snowshoes. An Indian will come with him to guide him through the deep snow. But we don't have a name for the baby yet, do we?"

"Can we name him after Maria's mother?" said Josette.

"We don't know your name," Edith said to Maria's mother.

"Ojibwe cannot tell anyone their name," Maria's mother said.

"I tell you my English name," said Maria. "I cannot tell you my Ojibwe name. That is against Ojibwe laws."

Maria's father said, "Our names are sacred, but when we take English names, we can tell them. I have never taken an English name. Only Maria has an English name in our family."

"Then why don't we name him after Maria? A name beginning with M," Josette suggested, holding Maria's hand.

Josette and Maria tried to think of all the boys' names that started with M. "Martin, Matthew, Maurice, Melvin, Michael, Miles, Morgan, Mortimer . . . "

"Stop," said Edmund. "I like Miles because we've come so many miles."

"I like that, too," said Edith. "That way we'll never forget our time here in the North."

"We must go now," said Maria's father.

"Please stay, just a little while, please," said Josette,

remembering the birchbark scroll. "Will you read the Indian scroll for us?"

"I will try," he said.

Josette ran to her room and brought the scroll to him.

He looked at it carefully, then smiled. "Yes, I can read it," he said.

Maria and Josette looked over his shoulder.

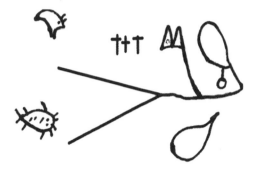

"This is a love letter from an Ojibwe girl to her lover. She is asking him to come to her lodge to visit her." He pointed to the crosses on the scroll. "The girl is a Christian, and she has two friends who are Christians." Then he pointed to the animal at the top of the scroll. "This is a bear, and the girl is of the Bear totem. That is important to know."

Then he pointed to the little triangles next to the crosses. "These are the lodges where the girls live, and next to the lodges is a big lake." He indicated the line at the top of the scroll and explained, "This is a trail which is well-traveled. The line that comes into the trail is the road leading to the lodges." His finger touched the small figure at the bottom of the scroll, the figure that looked like a fish. "This is the Mud Puppy totem. The lover is of this totem." Then he pointed back to the lodges. "You see the hand in the lodge?" he asked. They looked carefully and saw something resembling a hand. "That is the hand of the writer of the love letter. That tells him where she lives."

Josette and Maria were wide-eyed. They could hardly believe that many years before they came to Copper Harbor a young Indian girl had lived and had written a letter to the boy she loved, inviting him to visit her. Maria's father had opened up the scroll's meaning to them, letting them hear the voice of someone who lived long ago calling to her lover.

"I wonder if he visited her," Josette said.

"Did they get married?" Maria asked.

"We do not know," said Maria's father. "Maybe he wrote back to her, but this is the only scroll your friend found."

"Her love is still here," said Maria's mother. "Now we read about her love. I can feel her spirit in the room."

"We must go now," said Maria's father.

"Before you leave," Josette asked Maria's mother, "will you stop at the soldiers' quarters to see the wool from Mismatched, my sheep that was killed by a wolf? Private Wilks said that you might be able to make a blanket from it."

Maria's parents looked at each other. Maria's mother said, "I am not sure that I would be welcome there."

"Come with me," said Edmund. "I'll take you to the soldiers' quarters, and I'd like to introduce Maria's father to Captain Clary. He will want to know how you helped us on our mission to L'Anse. Then Josette and Maria and Maria's mother can look at the wool."

"And when you get back," said Edith to Edmund, "Miles will be awake and you can hold him."

While Josette, Maria, and Maria's mother went to the soldiers' quarters in search for Private Wilks, Edmund took Maria's father to Captain Clary. Captain Clary greeted Maria's father warmly. He was eager to meet him and to establish good relations with the neighboring Indians. Maria's father explained that soon they would be going on a hunting trip and that when they got back it would be close to Christmas.

"Then you must have Christmas with us here at the fort," said Captain Clary. Maria's father agreed to come and celebrate Christmas with the soldiers at the fort and with Father Baraga, and to attend the baptism of Miles.

"Now we must go," said Maria's father. "I feel a storm coming. The waters of the harbor will be very dangerous in a few hours."

In the soldiers' quarters Private Wilks had brought out the three pelts of wool for Maria's mother to examine. Josette didn't want to look at the ears of the sheep. "I will take the sheep's wool," said Maria's mother. "I can make the lining of a coat from this wool, and maybe even the lining of moccasins for when winter comes. But I will first make a little blanket for Miles."

Maria's father stopped for them at the soldiers' quarters, and they returned to the house and picked up their things, and then it was time to leave. While Edith and Edmund thanked Maria's mother and father again for all that they had done for them, Josette could hardly look at Maria. She couldn't say "Goodbye." The words stuck in her throat, but Maria whispered, "I will come once more before we leave for the hunting."

Then they were gone.

CHAPTER FIFTEEN

lightning

The storm came in the night. It raged all through the night. High winds played with the trees, breaking off crowns and splitting some trees in two. Lightning zigzagged down the sky. Thunder roared so close by that it woke up Miles, who began to cry.

Bright streaks of lightning illumined Josette's room, jolting her awake. She jumped up and looked out her window. She could see waves on the lake so high that water was sloshing in the two canoes on the shore and one of the canoes was swamped. The other one rose on a swell, turned over on its side, turned up again, and rode high on a wave. She watched as it was carried off into the middle of the lake. Then she lost sight of it. The sound of Lake Superior surf breaking on the rocks made it seem like the whole world was coming apart.

When she heard Miles crying, Josette went downstairs and found Edmund pacing the floor and Edith rocking the baby in her arms, singing a soft lullaby to him.

"This is the storm that Maria's father talked about," said Josette loudly. She had to talk loud over the wind that howled around the house, shaking the windows, and over the noisy rain that drenched the veranda and tried to creep under the door.

"I'm just thankful we got home on time," said Edmund. "Pity any poor sailor who's out there now."

"Isn't the *John Jacob Astor* due soon?" Edith asked Edmund.

"Any day now," he said.

"That's our ship," said Josette. "Maybe my sailor's on it."

"I'm not really worried about it," Edmund said. "She's a strong ship. We know that. We know how she handled storms."

"Isn't the *Astor* bringing us supplies?" asked Edith.

Edmund was reluctant to say yes. He knew what the ship was carrying to the fort—potatoes, beans, flour, yeast powder, lard, butter, sugar, salt, cornmeal, salt pork, sauerkraut, pickles, onions, vinegar, cheese, crackers, coffee, tea, dried fruit—items desperately needed now so that in the winter, when no ships could come into the harbor, the soldiers wouldn't starve. He wouldn't let himself think of the hunger that could come to the fort long before the Hunger Moon of February if this ship were lost in the storm and the supplies and sailors drowned.

By now it was morning, though it didn't look like morning. There was no light. Storm clouds black as night still swirled above their little house, but the rain had stopped. Gullie did not sing this morning. Just as Josette was saying, "I hope Gullie's safe," there was a sound like a knock on the door.

"Did you hear that knock?" Edith asked Edmund, "or was that the wind rattling the door?"

Edmund was already at the door. "Come in, come

in," he said. Dripping with water, there stood John Hayes.

"I've come for help," he said. "The *John Jacob Astor* is floundering on the rocks in the rough waters just inside the harbor. We're afraid she's sinking. She's carrying some men to work for me in the mines."

"I'll help, and I'll get soldiers to help, too," said Edmund.

"The waves are so high it's hard to see what's happening out there," said John Hayes.

"The *Astor* is carrying all our supplies," said Edmund. "Let's hope we can rescue the men and some of the cargo. The supplies are mostly in barrels. Let's hope the waves will push the barrels onto the shore."

"The ship arrived last night, but it was too dark for them to try to enter the harbor," said John Hayes, "and the storm was so fierce they had to wait outside the harbor until now."

"Didn't the Captain throw out the ship's anchor?" Edmund asked.

"It seems he did, but the wind changed direction during the night. The ship dragged her anchor, she couldn't hold, and the storm pushed her into the harbor where she most likely landed on rocks," said John Hayes.

"Didn't the Captain know how to prevent the anchor from slipping?" Edmund asked.

"This captain has been sailing on the *Astor* for ten years, ever since she was launched in 1834, but I suppose nothing like this has happened to him before. If anybody can save her now, that's Captain Benjamin Stannard," said John Hayes.

"Let's hope," said Edith.

As Edmund and John Hayes were leaving to get the soldiers, Josette said, "I'd like to come, too."

Edith began to say, "No, it's too dangerous—."

"If I go and it's too dangerous," said Josette, "I can go to the *Astor* to stay with François."

"Get dressed," said Edmund, "and maybe you can help. We'll all be pretty busy lighting fires to guide the sailors to shore, and when they get to shore, someone will have to help them get dried off and guide them to the *Astor*. You can take them to François, Josette."

"We'll need kindling wood to light fires on the shore," said John Hayes. "Do you have any extra kindling here?"

"I can put the kindling in a bag," said Josette, "while you're getting the soldiers."

"Good idea," said Edith. "I'll help."

When Edmund and John Hayes went to get the soldiers, who were just eating breakfast, Josette put on her raincoat, rain bonnet and boots. Edith said, "Be careful, Josette. But I'm glad that you can help."

They walked along the muddy trail to Copper Harbor, their feet often sinking in the mud. At certain low places swirling mud and water came up to their knees, but the rain had stopped. They heard the eerie sound in the distance, over and over again. It was the signal of a ship in distress.

At Copper Harbor miners were already lighting fires along the shore, although the fires were a little smoky because the wood was wet. "Look!" one of the soldiers called out suddenly. "Look, she's there, close to the island. Way out there!"

"I see her," yelled Josette. Her voice was carried away by the wind.

Josette took the bag of kindling to the soldiers and

the miners, who used it to light fires across the harbor to guide the ship. Some of the soldiers began to call out to the ship. "Oh-o-over here!" they shouted. "Oh-o-over here!" But the ship seemed to be heading straight for the biggest rocks.

Crack! Crack! Crack!

"They've hit a rock!" yelled Edmund. By this time everyone on shore could see the ship foundering on the rocks. In a few minutes, they heard an even louder C-R-A-C-K! "That's it," said Edmund. "They're aground." Waves washed over the ship. She began to tip on her side.

"Will the sailors drown?" said Josette.

"Let's hope not," said Edmund. "They seem to be getting into a lifeboat."

"Can't we help them?" said Josette.

"Not until they get to shore," said Edmund. "We can't send any canoes out in these big waves."

Watching from shore, peering into the distance, Josette could see some sailors clinging to big pieces of the wreckage. Some were hanging onto barrels. The wind was in their favor, fortunately. It was driving them into shore, not out into the lake. Other sailors were in a lifeboat and were trying to row toward shore, past the rocks and the shoals, and barrel after barrel seemed to be tumbling out of the ship and floating toward shore.

"Let's keep the fires going," said Edmund. "We can all help the sailors when they land on shore."

Josette kept close to the edge of Lake Superior with Edmund. He helped guide the lifeboat to shore, where the sailors and the miners who had come to work for John Hayes stumbled out, soaking wet from the spray and from the water that had almost swamped the boat.

They were shivering from the cold but thankful to have reached the shore alive.

Other sailors, still in the water clinging to pieces of wreckage, to twisted timbers and to barrels, were pushed toward shore by the waves. As they came in, one by one, the soldiers and miners on shore grabbed them and led them to the fires for warmth. Their teeth chattered. They were so cold they could hardly talk, but they muttered, "Thank you. Thank you." Josette's sailor was not among them, but maybe he hadn't sailed on this trip. She'd ask the captain later.

Finally the wind stopped howling. It sighed gently, and the wild waters of Lake Superior calmed down. Just then Josette, who was still looking out on the lake, caught sight of one last barrel that still had to come in. As it got closer to shore, the sailor on it seemed to be waving at her. Josette couldn't understand why the sailor would risk waving when he needed two hands to hang on to the slippery barrel. By now he was in shallow water and standing up, wading to shore. "Little lady!" he called out.

"It's my sailor!" said Josette, jumping up and down. "It's my sailor!" He was knee deep in water when Josette recognized him. "The one I didn't say 'Goodbye' to," she said.

"Well, now you can say 'hello,'" said Edmund.

"Hello," said Josette to the dripping, grinning sailor. "I'm so glad to see you!"

"I'm glad to see you, too," said the sailor. "No bears have eaten you," he joked, shivering.

"And no Indians have captured me," she joked back. "I have a lot to tell you."

"That will have to wait until we count all the men and your friend gets dried off," said Edmund. "We have to make sure that everyone was rescued, and we don't want anybody catching pneumonia."

Captain Stannard counted the men and breathed a sigh of relief when all were accounted for. Nobody had drowned. "Maybe I can still save the ship," he said, looking out into the distance to the abandoned ship lying tipped sidewise on rocks.

More and more barrels hit the shore. Some were stranded on rocks, and soldiers waded into the shallow water and retrieved them, stacking them on the shore.

"We'll have to leave the supplies here until we can get some wagons," said Edmund. "First we must take care of the men."

Josette took charge of her sailor, and the other sailors and the miners followed the two of them to the *Astor*, where François had hot chocolate waiting for them. Then François set the table with a sumptuous breakfast. At first the men were quiet. They ate the delicious food without talking, reflecting on how close they had come to death. Then, when they realized that they were alive and that no one had drowned, they began to talk, quietly at first, then boisterously.

Edmund and the soldiers stayed on shore long enough to put out the fires, then joined the sailors and miners at the *Astor* for breakfast. François told Edmund there wouldn't be room for all the sailors to stay in his place overnight. Edmund said to the Captain of the ship, "I'll take some of the sailors to the fort with me. We can put them up for a night or two, and they can eat with us."

"My men can stay with me," said John Hayes. "I'll take them to their quarters tonight."

The Captain thanked Edmund and told him that in a few days, provided that there were no more storms, the

Algonquin was due in Copper Harbor. "Then," he said, "my men can ride back to the Soo. Meanwhile, while we're waiting, I'd like to join my men at the fort."

"May my sailor stay with us?" Josette asked Edmund. She sat next to the sailor while he ate his breakfast, and François brought her a scrambled egg, a piece of toast, and a cup of hot chocolate. She had forgotten that she hadn't eaten breakfast before they came to rescue the men.

"Of course," said Edmund. "We have room for him."

"My name is Douglas White," he said, introducing himself to Edmund. "I'm originally from England, but now I live in Port Huron."

"Oh, Mr. White," said Josette. "Now I won't have to call you 'my sailor' any more!"

"I'd still like to be 'your sailor,'" he said. "I think I kept you from slipping off the deck of the *Astor*. That makes us friends forever."

The walk back to the fort was muddy and cold and wet. The sailors walked fast, eager to get warm. When they got to the fort, they saw that lanterns were lit to welcome them, and in the mess hall fires were roaring in the fireplaces and stoves. The smell of hot coffee penetrated the air.

After the soldiers brought dry socks, and even dry underwear and pants and shirts for the sailors, they all sat down to drink hot coffee together. When the sailors warmed up they began to tell about their scary night on Lake Superior. One said that last night's storm was more furious than any storm he had experienced on the ocean.

"What was worse," another sailor said, "is that between waves we could see the harbor where we had just been anchored, and we wondered if we'd ever see it again."

Another sailor said that there was nothing they could do to save the ship. They wondered if they would ever be able to forget the wrenching sounds of the ship breaking up. Each sailor said that he was thankful to be alive and safe and dry at the fort.

Dr. Isaacs came in and asked if anybody needed medical attention. They looked at each other and shook their heads "no." Everybody had survived without injury.

They had been awake and anxious all night and now they were warm and dry and no longer hungry. They soon began to yawn, and all agreed they could use some sleep. The soldiers offered them their bunks, and soon the soldiers' quarters were quiet. The soldiers tiptoed around, trying not to disturb the sleeping sailors.

Josette's sailor, Douglas White, did not go with the other sailors but accompanied her to the house. Edith, watching at the window for Josette, wondered who the sailor with her was. As soon as the two stepped up onto the veranda, Edith swung open the door and recognized the sailor immediately.

"This is Douglas White," said Josette, introducing him to Edith. "He was on the shipwreck."

"I remember you," Edith said. "Welcome to our house. Are you all right?"

"I'm fine," he said, "and I'm glad we could rescue most of the supplies."

"That's good news," said Edith.

By this time Edmund was back. He gave some of his own clothes to Douglas White while Edith and Josette hung Mr. White's wet clothes by the fire to dry. "We'll talk later," said Edmund. "Right now we'll get you a bed so you can get some sleep. You must be exhausted."

The next few hours at the fort were quiet ones. After the sailors woke up again and enjoyed another warm meal, their Captain took charge of them. He told Edmund that he'd like to take them back to the harbor to sort out the barrels and to help load the supplies on wagons.

"We'll get some planks to lay down over the deep muddy spots," said Edmund, "and then I think the wagons and horses will make it. The sooner the supplies dry out, the better."

All the sailors and a number of soldiers joined them on the walk back to Copper Harbor. Private Wilks drove one wagon, and Private Hawkins drove the other.

Josette was sorry to see Douglas White leave, but he assured her that as soon as they returned with the supplies, he wanted to hear all about her life at Fort Wilkins.

"Be careful for Indians," she called out to him as he left.

Douglas White laughed at her joke. "And you watch out for bears," he called back.

He didn't see the Indian girl hiding behind a tree waiting for the sailors to leave.

CHAPTER SIXTEEN

beaver

After the last man had disappeared into the woods, Maria edged out from behind a tree and looked around to make sure there were no sailors left at the fort. She wasn't afraid of the soldiers, but she wasn't sure about the sailors. She made her way to Josette's house and knocked on the door, quietly as usual. Josette recognized Maria's knock. She flung the door open and said, "You've come! You've come!" Then she remembered that Maria was leaving for two months and realized this was Maria's last visit for a long time.

"The waters are calm now, and there is no wind," Maria said. "My father wants to leave tomorrow morning."

"You promised to be back for Christmas," said Josette.

"We will keep our promise," said Maria. "But now we must get food for the winter months."

"How do you get your food?" asked Josette.

"We trap and hunt animals. And we fish," said Maria. "In a good hunt we come back with plenty of food and with beaver pelts and deerskins and rabbit fur, and...." Maria saw that Josette didn't like to think about killing animals. She explained, "It is the only way we can stay alive."

"Can you stay for dinner?" Edith asked, changing the subject. Edith held Miles up to Maria. "He's smiling at you. He wants you to stay. You were one of the first people to see him."

"I cannot stay," said Maria. "My mother and my father are waiting for me. They are packing for the trip, and I must help."

Josette didn't want to say goodbye and thought of something to delay the farewell. "Let's go to the bakery she said. "I'd like to give you a cookie before you leave."

"I have something for you, too" said Maria. "I hid it behind a tree."

The girls left the house together, Edith saying that she would pray for Maria and her parents while they were gone and asking to be remembered to Maria's mother. "We'll try to think of the wonderful Christmas we will have together when you get back," she said to Maria.

Edith felt sorry for Josette, losing her best friend. Her *only* friend her own age. Edith wondered how long she and Edmund and Josette would be staying at the fort. Since there was no sign of Indians wanting to attack the miners or soldiers, she could think of no reason for anyone to stay. The stories about the long, cold winter filled her with fear, especially for Miles and Josette. She wondered what the soldiers would do if they got snowed in and there was no place to go, with nights so long and days so dark.

Josette and Maria stopped at the bakery to see if there were any cookies. "When we saw you and Maria coming," the bakers said, "we put some cookie dough in the oven. The cookies will be ready in about a minute."

When the cookies came out of the oven, Josette noticed that they were bigger than usual. Then the bakers sprinkled precious extra sugar on two cookies and handed one to Maria and one to Josette. "We'll have plenty of cookies for you at Christmas," they said to Maria. "Be sure to come back."

"You make the best cookies," said Maria, thanking them. "Ojibwe do not make butter cookies."

The girls let the cookies cool to just the right temperature before eating them. A hot cookie burns the tongue, but a warm, buttery cookie melts in the mouth.

They walked together to the place where Maria had hidden her gift for Josette. When they got to the tree, they sat down and each ate her cookie. Eating the cookies together was the best part. Josette knew that for two months or more she would be eating cookies alone, without Maria, and Maria knew that she wouldn't be eating another butter cookie until Christmas.

Then Maria pulled something from behind the tree. (Josette was always amazed that Maria seemed to know each tree. To Josette one tree looked like another tree. There were only a few that she could tell apart.)

"These are snowshoes," Maria said. She handed them to Josette. "The snow is very deep here in winter. Maybe next week the snow will fly, and you will sink in the snow if you do not have snowshoes. On these you will glide over the top of the snow. My father made them for you. They are your size."

"Your father is very kind," said Josette. "When you come back, we can go snowshoeing together."

"And sliding on the ice," said Maria. "This little lake will freeze solid, and sometimes all of Lake Superior freezes over."

"Thank you," said Josette, running her fingers over

the smooth surface of the snowshoes. She held one up to her foot to test it for size. When she stood up on it, Maria had disappeared. She had slipped away. It was too painful to say "Goodbye."

As Josette was walking back to the house carrying her snowshoes, she thought she heard a loud whistling sound in the distance. "Did you hear that sound?" she asked Edith as she came back into the house.

"It sounds like a ship. Maybe it's the *Algonquin* coming into Copper Harbor," Edith said.

Not long after, Private Wilks came driving past the house in a wagon loaded with barrels. Josette followed him. He stopped at the quartermaster's building, and the soldiers who worked for the quartermaster began unloading the barrels immediately. The barrels were heavy from having been in water. Dripping water seeped from those that had not been sealed properly, meaning that the contents would be wet or at least damp. As soon as all the barrels had been unloaded, Private Wilks had to leave again to pick up more barrels at Copper Harbor. It would take many trips back and forth to unload them all.

Josette caught him just as he was turning his wagon around to head back along the trail. "Did you hear that horn?" she called out to him.

"Yes," he said. "We think it's the *Algonquin*. The sailors will be happy to see her. They want to get back to the Soo and to their families."

Josette entered the quartermaster's building to see what was in the barrels. The soldiers were trying to find barrels that contained perishable food. It was hard to identify them, but those barrels needed to be opened first so that the food wouldn't spoil.

When the first barrel was opened, a rancid smell

filled the air. The barrel contained potatoes, soggy and moldy. The soldiers took the potatoes out one by one, sorting good from bad. Many were squishy and leaked a putrid liquid when picked up. The soldiers' hands began to smell like rotten potatoes.

Many of the other barrels of potatoes were in better shape. Barrels of flour, sugar, cornmeal, salt and crackers had survived their bath in the water. Most of the other food had survived, also, although the dried raisins and dried apples felt moist and slightly sticky. At the bottom of one barrel of cornmeal, a soldier found a dead mouse, but he didn't show it to Josette.

Then another wagon pulled up, driven by Private Hawkins. As the barrels were being unloaded, Private Hawkins called out to Josette, "Look here. This barrel's addressed to 'Lt. Edmund Elliott and Family.'"

Josette went to read the label. The barrel had come all the way from Virginia. She couldn't wait to see what was in it. She hoped it wasn't potatoes.

"How will we get the barrel to our house?" she asked Private Hawkins.

"I'll drop it off on my way back to the harbor. There are still a lot of barrels down there, waiting to be picked up."

Edith was delighted. "We'll open it when Edmund gets back," she said. "It's from our sister. I hope there's some material for a new dress for you. And maybe some clothes for Miles."

"And maybe some molasses candy," said Josette. "Nice and chewy!"

They heard a knock on the door. It was John Hayes with his men. "I wanted to say hello and tell you we'll be working on the site of the mine just outside the fort," he said.

Josette was elated. "May I come and watch?" she said.

"If your sister says it's all right. Today we're going to map out the site. We won't be doing any blasting yet. But when we start to blast holes in the rocks, it will be too dangerous for you. After we're finished blasting and we've sunk a shaft in the mine, we'll see if you'd like to go down in the mine," John Hayes said.

"We'll see," said Edith.

Josette went with John Hayes and his men to the mine site. They marked the spot where they would blast the earth open with black powder. Mr. Hayes explained to the miners that once they had broken beyond the surface of the ground, they would bore into the rock with hand drills and sledge hammers. After that, they would tamp black powder into the holes and light fuses to explode the powder and open up the mine. Josette listened carefully.

"How deep will you dig," she asked, "and where will you put the dirt and the rocks?"

"What good questions, Josette," John Hayes said. "We'll go about forty feet deep at first. A lot depends on what we find. We may have to go as deep as 125 feet. If we find copper at forty feet, we'll blast tunnels horizontally. It's just like making rooms in a house. Oh, yes, and where will we put the dirt and rocks? We'll bring dirt and rocks up in buckets and make piles here, just outside the mine shaft."

Josette couldn't imagine what the shore of Lake Superior would look like with piles of dirt and rocks standing all over the shore. She could picture huge clumps of copper coming out of the earth. There would be a lot to watch. She was excited about going down into the mine, too. She couldn't wait to go beneath the surface of the earth. She didn't know how dangerous mines could be and that sometimes there were cave-ins and that often miners who were buried in cave-ins could not be rescued.

Despite her excitement over the mine, Josette noticed that the sun was moving rapidly across the western sky. She knew Edith would be looking for her, and Edmund and Mr. White would be coming with news of the *Algonquin*. There was also that barrel addressed to "Lt. Edmund Elliott and family," waiting to be unpacked.

When she got home, Edmund and Mr. White were already there. Edith was drinking coffee with them. Edmund said to Josette, "I suppose we should wait until after supper before we open the barrel?"

Josette knew that he was only teasing, and before she could reply, Edmund was already prying the barrel open.

They couldn't see what was in the barrel until Edmund removed the packing material on the top. Once that was removed, Josette saw something white, carefully folded. Edith lifted it out, "It's a baptismal dress," she said.

"There's a note pinned on it," said Josette.

The note said "Edith, this was Josette's dress when she was baptized. Now it's for your baby. It doesn't matter if it's a boy or a girl."

The little garment was beautiful. Edith remembered that their mother, hers and Josette's, had made it many years ago. She wiped her eyes. Then she said, "It will fit Miles when Father Baraga comes at Christmas." Underneath the baptismal dress were several hand-knitted suits for Miles.

"He'll soon be old enough to wear the suits," Edmund said.

"You lift out the next layer," Edith said to Josette. Josette lifted out beautiful cloth. "This is to make dresses for us," said Edith. It was soft, blue wool. It would keep them warm in winter, and the color would help them remember in the middle of winter that blue skies would come again.

"Now it's your turn," Edith said to Edmund. He lifted out hand-knitted socks. They were for him. The socks were wool, too, and would keep his feet warm in the snow.

The next layer was candles. "We'll need a lot of candles in the winter," Edith said.

Josette peered deep in the barrel. She saw food. "May I lift out the next layer?" she said. First she brought out a fruitcake. She held it up and thought she saw cherries and walnuts and raisins. Her mouth watered. Then there was gingerbread. Then molasses cookies. While Josette thought of how good these would taste, Edith pulled out two huge Virginia smoked hams.

"There isn't any better ham in the world," she said. "It will keep 'til Christmas, and then we'll share it with everyone at the Christmas dinner."

Next came a round wheel of cheese, but that wasn't the end. There were jars of oysters, pineapple, peaches and strawberry jam. There was black tea, just what Edith had been longing for. There were peanuts in the shell. And way at the bottom of the barrel was chocolate candy and molasses toffee.

Douglas White enjoyed watching them unload the barrel. "This feels like Christmas already," said Edith. "But I'm forgetting about you," she said to him. "I'll make us some supper, and we'll celebrate with black tea and fruitcake for dessert."

"I'd enjoy that," he said. "And while we're waiting

for supper, maybe the little lady will tell me all about the gull who followed her after she got off the ship. Did I just hear a gull nearby?"

In the excitement of opening the barrel, Josette had forgotten that Gullie had disappeared in the storm. She listened. Yes, it was coming from the roof. "Hiyah . . . hiyah . . . hiyah . . . yuk-yuckle-yuckle."

CHAPTER SEVENTEEN

winter

The sky was azure and the air crisp the following morning. Josette put on a sweater when she went outside after breakfast. She wanted to see the *Algonquin* sail into Copper Harbor. Edmund and Douglas White had already left, but Private Wilks was driving past her house in a wagon and invited her to ride with him. Edith gave permission.

"The sailors and some soldiers left early this morning," Douglas White told Josette, "and this is my second trip."

"Did the *Algonquin* come in already?" she asked.

"Long before you were up," he said.

"Do you think they'll be leaving today?" Josette asked.

Private Wilks looked at the sky. "I suppose they'd like to set sail before we get more storms," he said, "and I don't blame them."

"Do you wish you were going back with them?" asked Josette. "Where is your home?"

"I come from Kentucky. I joined the Army, and before I knew it, I was sent to build Fort Wilkins and to fight Indians."

"Don't you like it here?" Josette asked.

"I like it," he said, "especially since you're here. But I miss my little sister. She's about your age."

The ground had drained, and the mud ruts had dried, so the trip to Copper Harbor didn't take very long. When they arrived, soldiers and sailors were unloading the last of the cargo. Cargo from the ship was standing on the dock. Edmund came over to talk to Private Wilks, who had pulled up his wagon to help load up whatever was marked for Fort Wilkins.

"I'm glad to see that there are supplies for us," said Edmund. "We can use every supply we can get. Who knows when the next ship will come in?"

Captain John McKay of the *Algonquin* and Captain Stannard of the *John Jacob Astor* came over to talk to Edmund. Captain McKay said, "I want to get off by noon, if we can. When I saw the *Astor* out there stranded on rocks at the entrance to the harbor, I knew that the sooner we could get off, the better. We can't risk a storm like the one that grounded the *Astor*. It's amazing that they're all alive."

Captain Stannard said, "My men are all going with Captain McKay, but I decided to stay here to try to rescue the *Astor*. She's salvable, I think. I can't just leave her. The winter storms will pummel her to pieces."

Josette found Douglas White loading up Private Wilks's wagon. "You'll be leaving soon," she said to the former. "Will I ever see you again?"

"I hope so," he said, "but I won't be doing much sailing in winter. I'll be back next spring. Look for me on another ship."

By noon everything had been unloaded and the *Algonquin* left the harbor. Josette watched it leave, and

Douglas White waved to her. She waved back, even after she could no longer see the ship.

The next few days were quiet ones. Josette missed Maria and Douglas White. Edith suggested that she practice some Christmas songs on the piano to get ready for the big Christmas celebration. Gullie still came every morning. Josette watched the miners bringing in equipment to the mine site just outside the fort. She could still get close because they hadn't started blasting. After the blasting, she would go to look again if John Hayes said it wasn't dangerous.

Sometimes in her dreams Josette saw copper shooting sky-high out of the earth. She wondered if dreams of copper shooting up into the sky came through the hole in Miles's dreamcatcher. The dreamcatcher seemed to work. When Miles woke up, he was always smiling.

One night about a week after the *Algonquin* had sailed away from Copper Harbor and was safe at the Soo, the first snow came. It came when most people at the fort were sound asleep, gently at first, piling soft white flakes on the grounds. Only the soldiers on guard saw it drifting down. It was beautiful.

When the soldiers changed guard, the wind picked up, blowing snow in all directions. It swirled and created tunnels of snow on the fort grounds. By three or four o'clock in the morning, the gentle snowfall had turned into a blizzard, blotting out the buildings. Josette's house almost disappeared, and only the roof of the soldiers' quarters showed.

One of the soldiers on guard knocked at Edmund's door about five o'clock in the morning to warn him about the snow. Edmund was the only one in the house who heard the knock over the howling wind, and when he opened the door the wind hurled snow into the room along with the soldier. Snow swirled around on the floor. The soldier's uniform and his hat were white with it. When Edmund pulled his head back into the room, his hair and eyebrows were white, even though he had put his head out the door for only a second to welcome the soldier.

"I'm covered with snow, Sir," the soldier said. "It's going to be hard to get to headquarters in this storm. I can't see any other buildings from here. Even the roof of the mess hall is disappearing. I thought you might want to string ropes from building to building. Otherwise we'll get lost here on the grounds."

"Good idea," said Edmund. "The quartermaster has ropes just for this occasion."

Edmund put on his warmest coat and a cap that he pulled over his ears, then he wrapped a scarf around his face to keep his nose from freezing. He pulled on heavy boots. He wasn't sure the boots were high enough to keep him from sinking into deep drifts, but they were the best he had.

"The wind may knock us off our feet," the soldier warned.

"We can start by tying a clothesline around our waists to keep us together. Then we'll string it from a post on the veranda to the closest building, the company quarters. At least we have a start," said Edmund.

By now Edith had come downstairs. She was wearing a warm robe. "Can I help?" she asked. "Would you like coffee before you go out in this blizzard?"

"We can't wait," said Edmund. "We've got to get ropes between the buildings before we're all buried. We'll get breakfast and coffee in the mess hall."

Josette appeared as they were leaving. She looked

for Edmund and the soldier from the windows, but snow was sticking on the windows. They had turned completely white and blocked out all views, and she couldn't see a thing through them.

Edith said, "We must bring Miles's crib down here near the stove." She and Josette went upstairs to get the crib. Miles was still fast asleep. Edith lifted him out gently and put him on the bed. The wind created a chill in the bedroom, and she shivered. The dreamcatcher swayed in the breeze.

After they placed the crib near the warm stove, Edith brought Miles down. He was now wide-awake and hungry. "I'll feed him while you heat water for breakfast," she said to Josette. "Fortunately, we've got a good supply of wood to keep us warm."

The wind screeched around the corners of the house all morning. Josette tried to see the clothesline stretching from the veranda to the soldiers' quarters, but its color blended in with the snow. She could not see Edmund or the soldier, either.

"Don't worry," said Edith, "they can't get lost in the snow if they hang onto the ropes."

By noon the wind stopped howling and the snow stopped falling. Then, like a miracle, the sun came out.

"Look!" said Josette. "The windows are sparkling like stars!"

"I wonder if Edmund will come home for dinner," said Edith. "I suppose he'll be eating in the mess hall and stringing up ropes all day. I wonder how deep the snow is."

"Shall I open the door so that we can see out?" asked Josette.

"Just for a second," said Edith, who was as eager as Josette to see if the snow was too deep to walk in.

When they opened the door, a pile of snow fell into the room and covered the entrance to the house. Before they closed the door again, Edith tried to see the clothesline at the end of the veranda. She saw what she thought was the knot, but nothing else. They wiped up the snow, but Josette couldn't resist making a snowball out of the thick, packy snow. After a while, the snowball melted away in the kitchen sink. Josette wished she could go out and make more snowballs.

"Do you think I can go snowshoeing?" Josette asked. "It looks so beautiful, and Maria said that with snowshoes I can glide over the top of the snow."

"Not now," said Edith. "Edmund has a lot of work to do so we'll eat dinner without him, and when he gets back, we'll see what he thinks about snowshoeing. You can't go out alone."

Gradually the snow melted on the windows, and Josette was able to watch for Edmund. She could see the flagpole across the parade ground but the flag didn't billow. It seemed to be frozen stiff. She could see the roofs of the buildings outlined in snow and smoke snaking up out of the chimneys of the buildings. Only when it was beginning to get dark did she see Edmund, hanging onto the clothesline, making his way home.

"It's letting up," he said, stamping off snow at the door. "We've got ropes to all the buildings. I think we're safe. For now we've got plenty of wood, but we'll need a lot more once winter comes. As soon as we can get into the woods, I'll send soldiers out to cut down trees."

"I've got coffee ready for you," Edith said, "and then we'll have supper. It's been a long day for you. You must be tired."

"I am tired," said Edmund. "It's good to get out of the snow."

Josette didn't want Edmund to be too tired. "Do you think I could go snowshoeing after we eat?" she asked him hopefully.

"I don't know why not," he said. "By that time I'll be warmed up and rested."

The moon shone on their table, reflecting the light of the snow. Their house stood in a silver landscape. Edmund decided that it was too beautiful to stay indoors, and Edith helped Josette bundle up in a scarf and mittens and a cap covering her ears and pulled down to her eyes. Edmund helped her with the snowshoes. "Now let's see how they work," he said, getting dressed again himself in his outdoor clothes, dried by the fire.

At first Josette didn't know how to walk on top of the snow. Edmund steadied her when she was about to fall. He took her to the clothesline and told her to hang onto it. "Go easy, go light," he said. "Let the snowshoes work for you."

She caught on quickly. While she glided over the snow, Edmund trudged in it, hardly keeping up with her. "You can go in the house if you want to," said Josette. "It's so bright now, I can't get lost. I can see the fence of the fort. I'll stay in the grounds."

Edmund hesitated, but then he couldn't think of a reason not to let Josette snowshoe on her own. "All right," he said, "but only for half an hour. I'll time you, and Edith and I will watch you from the window."

"I'll go to the fence, first," she said, "and then I'll snowshoe around the buildings. Maybe the bakers are still in the bakery." She was thinking how good a sugar cookie would taste.

The snow stood in little mountains where the wind had sculpted it. and Josette snowshoed in the valleys between the snow mountains, gliding over the frozen surfaces. The whole world looked like diamonds. The moon made a moon path, like the moon path she had seen so many weeks ago when she had seen the wolf from her bedroom window. Hoping she would be able to talk to one of the guards, she stopped at the guardhouse.

"Hey, Josette," the guard called out to her, "how do you like the snow?"

"I love it!" she said. "I promised Edmund I'd stay on the fort grounds, though. I don't want to get lost in the snow."

"I wish I had a pair of snowshoes," the guard said. "Maybe I'll make myself a pair. Would you let me use yours as a pattern?"

"Yes," said Josette. "These are the best. My Ojibwe friend, Maria, gave these to me. Her father made them."

"Then they must be the best," said the guard.

Josette glided along the fence of the fort, feeling like the only person in the world. No one else was out. Then as she came to a break between buildings, she had the eerie feeling that someone was standing in the small clearing ahead. She moved toward it. Maybe one of the soldiers had snowshoes . She hoped to find a friend.

Suddenly she stopped. Standing in front of her, still at a distance, was a wolf, bathed in moonlight, just like the other wolf she had seen. It was beautiful, but she remembered the wolves that had killed Mismatched, and she turned around in a flash, snowshoeing so fast that she could hardly breathe. She didn't dare look back. She knew that the wolf could travel much faster than she could.

Finally, she was pounding on the door of her house. She almost fell into Edmund's arms when he opened the door.

"What's the matter?" he said. "I watched you, and you seemed to be enjoying yourself."

"There's a . . . wolf . . . in the fort." She could hardly speak. "There aren't any more sheep for him to eat."

"I'll get my gun," said Edmund. "We don't need hungry wolves chasing little girls."

"Oh, be careful, Edmund!" said Edith.

"Don't worry," said Edmund. "By tomorrow Josette will have a wolf rug."

"Oh, I hope not," said Josette. "I was scared, but he was beautiful in the moonlight. He was all silver."

Edmund came back in a short time. "I saw the tracks," he said, "but the wolf was gone. He was probably more afraid of you than you were of him."

The next morning Edmund and several soldiers followed the wolf tracks into the woods. They found the carcass of a deer. Only the bones were left. Scraps of bloody flesh dotted the trail to Lake Superior.

CHAPTER EIGHTEEN

bad

As the snow began to melt after the blizzard, there were bright, sunny days left in October for those living at Fort Wilkins. Even though night came earlier and earlier and brought a chill to late afternoon, the days were warm. Now the soldiers could go into the woods and cut down trees. All day Josette heard the sound of trees falling and of saws cutting them into logs. She heard the sound of logs being dragged into the fort grounds and the soldiers chopping them into wood for the fireplaces and stoves.

Sometimes she heard the sounds of guns being fired. Soldiers were out hunting for fresh meat. Their kill supplied the troops with venison, rabbits, ducks and geese. The cooks turned deer into a rich venison stew, and they roasted rabbits, ducks and geese over an open fire until the skin burst and crackled and turned a golden, mouth-watering brown.

For a few weeks there were only snow showers. Temperatures by day stayed mild, so lakes did not freeze, and ice did not form. Soldiers were assigned to fishing. Private Wilks and Private Hawkins caught trout and whitefish from the two canoes. Often they set out a net overnight and caught seventy fish by the next morning. Josette helped count the fish. Sometimes Private Wilks stopped in for a cup of hot chocolate when he brought trout to Josette, Edith and Edmund. He was amazed at how fast Miles was growing.

The mine site was out of bounds for Josette now that John Hayes and his men had begun the blasting. All day long Josette could hear the thunderous sound of shattering rock. Sometimes she thought she felt the earth trembling under her feet. She couldn't wait to see how deep the hole was and to go down into the earth. Edmund assured her the miners were making good progress and in a few weeks they'd be bringing up copper. Edith really didn't want Josette going down in a mine, but Edmund had told her that this was a once-in-a-lifetime experience. He admitted that he would like to go down, too, and look around in the earth. Now Edith had another thing to worry about. She didn't want to lose a sister or a husband.

Soon it was November. Snow began to fall again, and ice formed a thin skin on the sides of the lakes. It snowed every day, but so far there were no more blizzards.

Although Edmund kept the soldiers busy by day, the nights in their quarters were long. Some of the soldiers read books. Some played cards. Some whittled and carved gifts for Christmas. Many wrote letters. Since the mail came by dog train from Green Bay, Wisconsin every two weeks, the soldiers wanted to make sure their letters reached home before Christmas. They also hoped to receive letters, or maybe even packages, from home. Mail call was one of the best times at the fort. Letters from home could lessen the loneliness beginning to settle into the hearts of the men so far away from home.

Then one night, just after she had been asleep for a while, Josette woke up to noisy sounds. Not the sounds of logging or mining but more like the sounds of human voices. Shouts. She hoped soldiers weren't yelling at Indians.

Edmund was already up and shutting the door as Josette came down the steps. "What's wrong," she asked Edith, who was pulling on her robe.

"It sounds like there's a fight in the barracks," Edith said.

"Are they fighting each other?" Josette said.

"I don't know," said Edith, "but it sounds like they're drunk."

"How did they get drunk?" said Josette.

"I'm not sure," said Edith, "but last night after you went to bed, we heard a dog team coming into the fort. Edmund thought it might be miners visiting the fort for a card game. Apparently they got past the guards. It was quiet for a long time. We went to bed. Suddenly we heard yelling, and Edmund got up to investigate."

As they looked out the window, Josette could see lanterns being lit in the soldiers' quarters, and she heard Edmund giving orders. His voice was stern. In a few minutes she saw soldiers leading other soldiers into the jail. Edmund and Captain Clary followed. Then she saw Private Wilks and Private Hawkins leading two soldiers to the hospital, where Dr. Isaacs, who had heard the commotion, already had lanterns glowing. Edith said, "Those two men must be injured."

Josette and Edith couldn't get back to sleep. They waited for Edmund to come home, though he was gone a long time.

As he opened the door, Edmund said, "What a

night! I think we've got things under control now."

Josette had never seen Edmund look so disgusted.

"What happened?" Edith said.

"That dog team we saw coming into the fort last night brought men with gallons of whiskey to sell. Bringing liquor into the barracks is forbidden, but some of the soldiers bought whiskey and couldn't stop drinking. Then they got into fights. Captain Clary and I took the troublemakers to the jail. They're going to spend the night there to sober up."

"What about the two soldiers who went to the hospital?" asked Josette.

"One has a bloody nose. He had blood dripping all over his uniform. The other one injured his thumb fighting. I hope the thumb isn't broken. Those two are going to spend the night on hospital cots."

"We saw you and Captain Clary rolling something to the woods behind the hospital," Josette said. "What was that?"

"We seized 250 gallons of whiskey, opened the cask and poured the whiskey down the hill," he said. "All 250 gallons. By now it should have been absorbed by the earth."

"What happened to the men who brought in the whiskey?" asked Edith.

"When they saw us coming, they took off in a hurry. It was too late to catch up to them and arrest them. Who knows where they are by now? If they want to sell liquor in Copper Harbor, that's one thing. But no one brings liquor into the barracks and sells it to my men," said Edmund. "If I ever see those whiskey sellers here again, I'll arrest them on the spot."

"We've got to help the men find things to do at night," said Edith.

"Let's talk about that in the morning," said Edmund. "Morning will be here soon enough."

It was hard to get back to sleep. Josette had never seen anyone drunk. She liked all the soldiers, and she was sorry that some were in jail and in the hospital. She tried hard to think of what she could do to help them. Then at last she fell asleep.

The next morning early Edith and Edmund were already up and just beginning breakfast when Josette came down. "I have an idea," Edith was saying. "Why don't I start a choir? I'm sure there are a lot of good voices here at the fort, and those who can't sing can do other things to prepare for Christmas."

"I can help," said Josette. "I can play the piano for the choir."

Edmund beamed. "What a good idea," he said. "If the soldiers like the idea, I'll have them move the piano to the mess hall. That's a good place to practice. Is that all right with you?"

"For the duration," she said. "Josette and I can practice over there by day while the soldiers are at work. Then at night we can train the choir. We'll try to prepare a Christmas program. And maybe we can sing and play favorite songs of the other soldiers in the barracks to cheer them up."

"I have an idea, too," said Josette. "We can start a newspaper."

"Another good idea," said Edmund, "all born from a nasty drunken night. I'll tell the soldiers about these two ideas this morning—after I talk to them about what happened last night."

"Will they get out of jail today?" Josette said.

"We'll see what Captain Clary says, but I suppose there's no point in keeping them in jail any longer,"

Edmund replied thoughtfully. "There's work to be done today. For one thing, we need a lot more firewood."

"What about the men in the hospital?" Edith asked.

"I'll talk to Dr. Isaacs. If he says they're all right, they can come back and get to work, too," said Edmund. "It looks like I have a busy day ahead." Then he left.

As Edith bathed and fed Miles, she sang to him. She was happy thinking about starting a choir, and in her mind she got out all her pieces of choral music. She would have to test the soldiers' voices and select not only tenors and basses but also those who could sing the soprano and alto lines. She hummed a few songs as Miles fell asleep in her arms, one of which Josette recognized as "My Country 'tis of Thee." She knew how to play that patriotic hymn and thought how beautiful it would sound in four-part harmony with men's voices.

Josette cleared the breakfast table, washed and dried the dishes, made the beds and thought about a newspaper. If Edmund agreed, maybe she and Private Wilks could be the editors, and she could interview soldiers for the paper. She thought the men might like to talk about their homes and the places they came from. They might even like to write their own stories. Maybe Edith would write a story about how Maria's mother had delivered Edith's baby, too. The more Josette thought about the newspaper, the more excited she got. She thought there might be more stories in the fort than the paper could hold!

The newspaper would have to be printed by hand, as they had no other way they could make copies. Making hand-printed copies would require the work of many soldiers, and she would have to find those who were good at printing legibly and neatly.

There was a knock at the door. It was Private Wilkins. "We've come to get the piano," he said. "We're taking it to the mess hall."

Edith said happily, "The soldiers must have liked the idea of singing in a choir for a Christmas program."

"Yes, Ma'am," said Private Wilks. "We've already got volunteers."

Outside stood the wagon, and two soldiers were placing planks to wheel the piano aboard. One of them said to Edith, "I'm a tenor. I used to sing in my home church choir."

"That's wonderful," said Edith.

"We can sure use some music up here," the soldier said. "We wouldn't have had that fight in the barracks last night if we'd been singing."

Josette told Private Wilks about her idea for a newspaper. He liked the idea.

"Who would be the editor?" he asked.

"Do you think we could edit the paper together?" she said. "Even though I'm only ten, I can write stories about how Maria found me."

"Co-editors," he said. "I think we'll make a great team."

"What about a name for the paper?" Josette asked.

"How about *The Fort Wilkins Agate*?" suggested Edith.

"Agates," Private Wilks said, "the beautiful stones on the shore of Lake Superior. I have a few agates I've picked up on the shore. I like to rub them until they gleam. One looks like it has clouds floating in it."

"I've got a couple agates, too," said Josette.

"That name for the paper will remind our readers of beautiful clouds floating in a bright blue sky," said Private Wilks.

"So will their own stories and their own music," Edith said.

CHAPTER NINETEEN

sing

The soldiers' quarters came alive in December. As the days grew shorter and the nights grew longer the snow fell every day, blotting out the paths and making every surface smooth and white. The soldiers ignored the dark nights and the weather and started preparing for the great Christmas celebration.

Just as Edith had predicted, many of the soldiers were good singers, and they were eager to join a choir. The group met every night in the mess hall for practice. Josette played the piano accompaniment. The soldier who had moved the piano proved to be the best tenor, and Edith gave him the tenor solo parts. Often Edith wrapped Miles up in blankets and carried him over to the mess hall with her. The baby loved the music and cooed along. He wanted to sing, too.

Many of the soldiers started making Christmas decorations. Some carved candleholders out of wood. The soldiers decided they would need many candleholders for the big Christmas spruce tree they were planning to cut. They wanted the tree to be aglow with candlelight. Some of them went out into the woods on moonlit nights, looking for just the right tree for Christmas. When they found it at last, they notched the trunk so they would be able to find it again.

Some of the soldiers were carving a crèche. This required delicate work to include the Baby Jesus and Joseph and Mary and the shepherds and the wise men and all the animals in the stable. Others worked on presents for friends, keeping their projects as secret as they could in their quarters.

The bakers promised to make special holiday cakes and cookies, and the cooks promised the best meal they could prepare. The cooks recruited soldiers several days before Christmas to hunt for ducks and geese and turkeys, rabbits, squirrels and deer. Lamb was also on the menu, and Edith contributed her smoked hams from Virginia.

Josette and Private Wilks sat down together at the kitchen table to plan the newspaper, starting with an outline and a list of articles they wanted to include. They agreed that the paper should include interviews with soldiers from different parts of the country telling about the places they came from. There might also be stories from soldiers writing about themselves and their life here in the frozen North. Josette assigned herself the story about how Maria rescued her from bears, and she and Private Wilks asked Edith to write about how Maria's mother helped deliver Miles. They decided to ask several soldiers to write about the first Christmas at Fort Wilkins, including an interview with Father Baraga. Josette and Private Wilks were sure that they could fill eight pages and that they would be working on the paper long after Christmas.

Josette was so busy playing the piano for the choir and planning the newspaper and knitting a red scarf for Maria that she almost forgot about Gullie until

Edith observed one morning that Gullie wasn't waking anybody up in the mornings any more. Edmund said, "Gullie's probably gone south for the winter."

"Will he come back in spring? " Josette asked.

"He's the most faithful gull I've ever seen," said Edmund. "You just wait until spring, and I'm sure he'll be back. He found you when you were lost. He'll find you again. By the time he comes back, he'll probably have his grown-up white and gray feathers."

"And his gold beak with the red dot," said Josette.

Josette counted the days to Christmas. On the fifth day before Christmas Maria had still not come. Josette was worried. Would Maria and her father and mother come on Christmas Eve for the celebration and on Christmas Day for dinner? They had been specially invited by Captain Clary and had promised to come. Where were they?

When was Father Baraga coming? Would he make it all the way from L'Anse in the deep snow?

Two days before Christmas Josette watched the soldiers cut down the Christmas tree. They pulled it out of the woods and shook off some of the snow before dragging it into the mess hall. Snow still rode on all the branches of the big spruce, the tallest Christmas tree Josette had ever seen. There was just enough room at the top for an ornament without bumping the ceiling. A stand that the soldiers had carved was waiting for the tree, and by the time the snow melted from its branches, the tree was standing tall again, making the otherwise bare mess hall look like a festive Christmas room.

Edith supervised the tree decoration. First the candleholders were fastened to the branches. The tree was so tall that one soldier had to stand on a ladder to put the top candleholders in place. Each holder held a small white candle that Josette and Edith had cut from big candles. The candles would all be lit on Christmas Eve. Before the soldier came down from the ladder, he put an angel on the top, hand-carved by one of the soldiers. The angel smiled down at this mess hall deep in the snow of northern Michigan.

Next, several soldiers brought ornaments they had made. Balls, stars, reindeer, a bear, cardinals and doves, a seabird that looked like Gullie—even a little porcupine with outstretched quills.

When Josette went to bed that night after choir practice, she saw a bright moon shining into her room, and she prayed that Maria and her mother and father would be guided by the light of the moon and that Father Baraga hadn't gotten lost in the woods somewhere between L'Anse and Fort Wilkins or been attacked by hungry wolves.

The morning of Christmas Eve dawned bright and clear. Just after dawn came a knock on the door. Edmund was greeted by a cheerful soldier, and Josette heard him say, "Father Baraga arrived a few minutes ago. He came with an Indian guide. They'll be eating breakfast with Captain Clary and staying in his house."

Then Josette heard Edith's voice. "Thank God," Edith said, "we'll have a Christmas Eve celebration and a baptism on Christmas Day!"

Josette heard the door close. She was happy to hear that Father Baraga had arrived, but the soldier hadn't mentioned Maria. Now Josette transferred her fear of wolves from Father Baraga to Maria. She pictured Maria and her mother and father asleep somewhere on the hunt and wolves coming silently into their tent and devouring them, just the way they had devoured Mismatched. It was a gloomy way to start Christmas Eve.

Edith could sense that Josette was troubled. Without asking what the trouble was, Edith said, "Don't worry. Maria promised to be here for Christmas Eve, and Maria always keeps her promises."

After their midday meal, the soldiers prepared the mess hall for the evening celebration. Dinner was scheduled for 7 o'clock, and after dinner there would be festivities.

Seven o'clock arrived, and still no Maria. Josette, Edith and Edmund, who carried the bundled-up Miles, walked over to the mess hall. A brilliant moon lit their path. Lanterns gleamed in all the windows. Edmund opened and closed the door to the mess hall quickly so as not to let in the cold. Standing behind the door was Maria. "You've come, you've come!" Josette said over and over again.

Edith and Edmund welcomed Maria's mother and father and led them to the special seats Edith and Josette had set for them. Maria sat next to Josette, and her mother and father sat across from Edith and Edmund.

Then Father Baraga came in with Captain Clary. In unison the soldiers called out, "Welcome, Father Baraga!"

He smiled, put his hands up in benediction, and said, "May God bless us all on this Christmas Eve."

The Christmas Eve meal was a simple one, although there were cookies for dessert. The big dinner would come on Christmas Day. When the meal was finished and the tables cleared, it was time for the celebration to begin.

Captain Clary stood up and said, "It's time for the lighting of the candles." Soldiers jumped up from the tables and volunteered to light the candles. There was silence in the hall while each candle was lit and everybody in the hall watched the tree come alight.

Captain Clary introduced Edith as the person responsible for the celebration. Edith stood up and the soldiers cheered. She went to the piano with Josette and announced, "My sister, Josette, will accompany us on all the songs." The soldiers cheered again, and Josette bowed. "Now," said Edith, "let's sing one song together, and then the choir will sing for us. Does everybody know 'Hark, the Herald Angels Sing?'"

As they nodded, Josette began to play. Edith led them in the words

> Hark, the herald angels sing,
> Glory to the newborn king.
> Peace on earth and mercy mild,
> God and sinners reconciled.
> Joyful, all ye nations rise,
> Join the triumph of the skies,
> Hark the herald angels sing,
> Glory to the newborn king.

Edith had tears in her eyes. She couldn't believe such music could arise from a mess hall in the frozen North. She beckoned to the private with the sweet tenor voice, whose name was Private Jones, to sing the second stanza alone. The soldiers joined in on the chorus, and the angel on top of the tree looked down on them and smiled.

Then the choir came up front to sing. The first song they sang was "While Shepherds Watched Their Flocks by Night." Even though Josette was playing the piano, she couldn't help thinking of Mismatched, who had died while nobody was watching her. The next song they sang was "Oh God, Our Help in Ages Past."

Many of the soldiers remembered this hymn from their churches back home.

Edith said, "We have a song that we want to dedicate to our Objibwe friends. Will they stand?"

That took Maria and her mother and father by surprise. As they rose, the soldiers clapped. "This song," said Edith, "will be sung by Private Jones, and the choir will join in the chorus. After we sing it, you may all join in the chorus of the second stanza."

Josette played an introduction to the song. Private Jones sang:

'T was in the moon of winter time,
When all the birds had fled,
That mighty Gitchi Manitou
Sent angel choirs instead;
Before their light the stars grew dim,
And wond'ring hunters heard the hymn:
Jesus your King is born,
Jesus is born,
In excelsis gloria.

Within a lodge of broken bark
The tender Babe was found,
A ragged robe of rabbit skin
Enwrapped his beauty round.
But, as the hunter braves drew nigh,
The angel song rang loud and high,
Jesus your King is born,
Jesus is born,
In excelsis gloria.

Maria's father cleared his throat. "I thank you," he said. We thought the fort was our enemy, but now we are friends. Our little girls, Maria and Josette, brought us together. We live in peace."

Captain Clary stood up. "We thank you for coming," he said. "We live in peace." He walked over and shook Maria's father's hand.

In the silence that followed, Edith motioned to Josette to play the piano. She played "Glory to Thee, My God, This Night." The choir sang, first the soprano line, then the alto line, then the tenor line, and then the bass. They sang it as a round. Soon everyone caught on and joined them. They finished the song by repeating the first stanza:

> Glory to Thee, my God, this night,
> For all the blessings of the light,
> Keep me, oh keep me, King of Kings,
> Beneath thine own almighty wings.

When the basses finished with the last line, "Beneath thine own almighty wings," peace settled over the room.

Captain Clary asked Father Baraga to say a few words. The priest, who had come on snowshoes in the deep dark of winter all the way from the comforts of L'Anse to a remote fort at the tip of the Keweenaw Peninsula, talked to the soldiers as though they were all his sons. He talked to them of the loneliness each one of them felt living away from those they loved. He told them that he often was lonely in a strange country far from his native Slovenia. He told them that Jesus must have been lonely, too, being so far from his Father and from his heavenly home. Then he told them to look up at the angel on the tree and at the stars and planets outside and to remember that no one was ever alone after that first Christmas Eve. He walked over to the crèche on the mantle of the big fireplace and said "Peace on earth, good will to men." He lifted his hand in benediction.

As soon as Father Baraga finished speaking, the choir started singing "My Country 'Tis of Thee." The soldiers leaped to their feet and joined in. They sang as though their hearts were bursting with joy.

Then the program was over.

Everyone stood around talking. No one wanted to leave. Josette asked Maria to stay overnight with her, and Maria's mother and father gave their permission. Edith asked the parents to stay, also, but they said they would go back to their wigwam. They had snowshoes and it was a perfect night for snowshoeing. The moon and stars would light their way. They promised to be back in the morning for the baptism of Miles and for Christmas dinner.

The soldiers left the mess hall humming. The last words Josette heard as they left the hall were the last lines of

> Glory to Thee, my God, this night.
> Keep me, oh keep me, King of Kings,
> Beneath thine own almighty wings.

CHAPTER TWENTY

christian

Christmas Day dawned clear and bright. Edith and Captain Clary had planned the day, with the baptism of Miles set for noon and dinner to follow immediately after. The candles on the Christmas tree would be lit again for the baptism and the dinner, and the mess hall would stay open all day so the soldiers wouldn't have to return to their quarters where they might feel lonely. Edith had asked Private Wilks and Private Hawkins to organize afternoon games.

Josette and Maria went snowshoeing after breakfast while Edith prepared Miles for his baptism. By the time they got back, the baby was wearing his long baptismal dress. Edith wrapped him in blankets, and Edmund carried him through the snow to the mess hall.

Father Baraga greeted them as they entered and led them to the front of the mess hall where a pure white bowl, filled with water that had been ice the night before, stood on the corner of a table. He asked Josette to play "Joy to the World" while the soldiers were coming into the mess hall.

The first soldiers to arrive lit the candles on the tree. When she saw others arriving, Josette began to play, and the soldiers hummed along with "Joy to the World" while they found their seats at the dinner table.

When everyone was ready, it was time for the baptism.

Father Baraga talked about the sacrament of baptism, and he said how special it was to baptize a baby on Christmas Day. Then he dipped his hand in the bowl. As he sprinkled water on Miles's head, he said, "I baptize thee, Miles, in the name of the Father, and of the Son, and of the Holy Ghost. Amen." He looked out into the mess hall at all the soldiers and the Indians and said, "Glory to God in the highest, and on earth peace, good will toward men." He asked everyone in the mess hall to shake hands with those nearby and to say "Peace."

A few soldiers walked up to Maria's mother and father, shook their hands and said "Peace." It seemed strange to Josette that the people who were supposed to be fighting each other were saying "Peace" to each other, but it seemed wonderful, too. Some important people in Washington had heard the word 'war' and had sent troops up here to fight the Indians. Josette wished that those people in Washington could be there in Fort Wilkins to meet Indians like Maria and her mother and father and the Indian guide with Father Baraga.

When the cooks heard the word "Peace," they and their helpers started carrying in huge platters stacked high with food. There were platters of mashed potatoes and sweet potatoes whipped with butter, and there were big bowls of gravy. There were turnips and cranberries, and there were no peas. Everyone gasped when the roast turkeys were brought in. They were beautifully browned, with skin and drumsticks looking so succulent that every mouth began to water. Then came platters of rabbits, squirrels, ducks, geese, deer and lamb, and thin slices of Edith's ham for everybody. The bakers brought in biscuits fresh from the ovens, so light and fluffy and warm that butter melted in them as soon as it touched the split open halves.

Everyone began to eat, and the first few minutes were quiet ones. Then conversation began to flow.

Josette and Maria had two months' catching-up to do. They talked between mouthfuls. Josette did not eat any lamb but enjoyed the other good dishes. Soon soldiers were bringing in dessert, huge cakes with sparkling white frosting. Edith wondered how they had managed to find enough white sugar for the frosting, heaped up like snow on the cakes.

After dinner Father Baraga said goodbye to everyone. He had to get to Eagle Harbor before nightfall to conduct a Christmas service in the little church there. Edith and Edmund thanked him, and Josette and Maria waved goodbye to him and his Indian guide as they left the entrance to the fort.

Edith and Edmund invited Maria and her mother and father to join them at the house for a small party. Maria's father said they could come for a little while, but then they'd have to get back to their wigwam. He told them that the hunt had been poor and that was the reason they had stayed away so long. He had only a few animal pelts and some deer and moose meat, so they would be getting ready to leave and go to L'Anse to live in a wooden house for the winter. "I will hunt there, and Maria can go to school."

Josette and Maria raced ahead of everybody back to the house. They had heard Maria's father talk about moving to L'Anse, and they didn't want to waste a minute of their short time together. Josette was already planning how she and Maria could go snowshoeing, maybe even sliding on the ice that was getting thick on the lake. They waited impatiently at the door for the others to return. Josette was eager to give her gift to Maria.

As the adults entered the house, Edith said, "Let's put candles on *our* Christmas tree." This was a surprise! Josette hadn't seen Edmund cutting down a small tree for them. She didn't know that Edith had brought enough candleholders from Virginia to put on another tree.

When Miles had been fed and had fallen asleep in his cradle near the fire, Edmund explained to Maria and her mother and father, "We give gifts on Christmas."

"Yes," said Maria's mother, "we know. Father Baraga told us when we lived in L'Anse."

"May I give my gift to Maria first?" asked Josette.

"Of course," said Edith.

"I made something for you," Josette said to Maria. She handed her a bright red scarf.

Maria wrapped it around her throat. It hung down almost to her knees. "Oh, thank you!" said Maria. "I shall wear it all winter. I have something for you, too."

She handed Josette a pair of deerskin moccasins. They were lined with sheepskin.

Josette slipped them on. "Thank you!" she said. "They fit perfectly!" She walked around the house showing off her present, and everyone laughed. They knew how much Josette loved this gift from her best friend.

"We have something for Miles," said Maria's mother. She handed Edith something soft and white. It was a woolen covering for his cradle.

"It's made from the wool of our sheep," said Edith. She stroked it. "It's beautiful. I will always remember you. You were here when I needed you. You delivered Miles." Edith's voice trembled. Then she said, "I have something for you, too." She went to her cupboard and brought out something wrapped in soft cloth.

Maria's mother unwrapped the object. It was a beautiful silver serving spoon.

"This was my grandmother's silver spoon," said Edith. "She gave it to me when I was a little girl. Her mother gave it to her. I want you to have it to remember us."

"Thank you," said Maria's mother, admiring the shiny silver. "It is the most beautiful spoon I have ever seen. I will think of you when I use it to serve rabbit stew. No Ojibwe woman has a spoon like this."

"Now we must go," said Maria's father.

"When can Maria come again?" Josette asked him.

"Not until the Grass Moon," said Maria's father. "Soon we shall go to L'Anse and live in a little wooden house in the Snow Moon and the Hunger Moon and the Crow Moon. Maria must go to school. White teachers help Maria learn English better."

"All is changing for Ojibwe," said Maria's mother. "Maria will have to live in the white man's world."

"Are we never coming back?" asked Maria.

"We don't know," said Maria's father. "Maybe we stay in L'Anse."

"Then I'll come to see you," said Josette. "Edmund will bring me."

Edmund looked at Maria's father. They both knew that Edmund could never make the trip without an Ojibwe guide. All Edmund could say was, "We'll see."

It would have been a tearful goodbye for Josette and Maria if there hadn't been a knock at the door just then. Edmund opened the door to greet a soldier who saluted and said quickly, "A man has fallen into Lake Superior. A couple of us were out stretching our legs, and we decided to walk on the lake. The ice seemed strong. We were sliding, he got ahead of us, and then he fell through. We've rescued him, but it took a little time. We brought him to the hospital, but he can't stop shaking from the cold. Dr. Isaacs is warming him up now. We don't want him to catch pneumonia."

"Who is it?" asked Edmund.

"It's Private Jones."

"No," said Edith, "not our tenor!"

"Private Jones asked if you would come and help him," the soldier said to Edith.

Josette and Edmund set out to accompany Maria and her mother and father to the entrance of the fort as Edith said goodbye, thanking them for coming and then hurried in the direction of the hospital. Josette was wearing the snowshoes Maria had given her, and Maria was wearing the red scarf from Josette. Maria had tied the scarf on over her fur parka.

It was hard to say goodbye.

"Write me a letter," Josette called out as Maria glided away.

"Letters do not travel well in winter," Maria called back.

"Hurry," urged Maria's father.

The last thing that Josette saw was Maria's red scarf against the white snow.

"You go back to the house and check on Miles," said Edmund. "I'll go to the hospital to look in on Private Jones."

Josette found Miles fast asleep. The house felt empty. Christmas was over, Maria was gone, and it would be three months before she would see her again. If then—.

When Edmund returned alone, he said, "Private Jones has a chill. Dr. Isaacs is hoping he won't catch pneumonia, so Edith is feeding him warm broth. He's shaking so much he can't hold a spoon."

After a while, Edith came back smiling. "He's going to be all right. He's stopped shaking, and Dr. Isaacs is watching over him. I'll go back in a few hours. Maybe by that time he'll be singing."

"This has been quite a Christmas," said Edmund. "I can't remember a better one, not even in Virginia. Who would have thought that Christmas could be so beautiful this far from home? Thanks to you both."

Edith said, "We'll never forget that Miles was baptized on Christmas Day."

Josette was parading around the house in her moccasins. They kept her feet warm. "I think I'll wear them in bed tonight," she said.

CHAPTER TWENTY-ONE

girl

One morning in January, John Hayes knocked at the door. "I've come to tell you that we're finishing up our work at the mine," he said. "We've mined about forty tons of black oxide, testing out at about eighty percent copper. That was good, but the copper's failed at a hundred and twenty-five feet, and we're not going any deeper."

"So are you leaving the mine?" Edmund asked.

"Yes," answered John Hayes simply. "In November I discovered what looks to be the richest copper on the peninsula. We're calling it the Cliff Mine. The mountain seems to be almost solid copper."

"May I go down in this mine before you close it?" Josette asked.

"That's why I'm here," said John Hayes. "You're invited too, Lieutenant Elliott."

"This is probably the only time in our lives that we'll go down into a mine," said Edmund, looking at Edith.

"Is it safe?" Edith asked.

"We've reinforced it with cedar beams so there's no chance of a cave-in. I'll only take you as far down as the first level. After your visit, we're picking up our equipment and moving out. If we wait until spring, melting snow could flood the mine, and we wouldn't be able to get down at all."

Josette already had her coat on. "I'm ready," she said, pulling on her boots.

Edith made no further objections, realizing this was an important opportunity for Josette and Edmund. As they left, though, she gave each of them a special hug.

At the entrance to the mine was a sign, *Pittsburgh and Boston Company.* Mr. Hayes shoveled away the snow that partly blocked the entrance. Then he gave Edmund and Josette each a hat and a candle set in clay.

"We always use candles to see if the air is pure enough to breathe," he explained, "and to light the place where we're working. That's the way our miners work, mostly by candlelight. If the candle goes out, we leave in a hurry! When we get down below, you can stick the candle into a timber while we look around." He lit a candle for himself as Josette looked down into the pit. She stood on the edge of the gaping hole, trying to see the bottom of the mine. All she saw was blackness and a few red-gold gleams in the sides. She looked around for ladders. She didn't see any. "How will we get down?" she asked Mr. Hayes.

"We'll hop into this kibble," he said, pointing to a large basket. "This is how we lower the miners and how we get the copper up here."

"Is that strong enough to hold us?" Josette asked him.

"You'll go down with me," said Mr. Hayes, "and Lieutenant Elliott will come in the second trip."

Josette knew that if she was with Mr. Hayes, she would be safe. Mr. Hayes went first and reached out for

Josette, half lifting her. She held her candle. It glowed in the dark. When they reached the bottom of the mine, Mr. Hayes lifted her down. Her candle was still glowing. Then he sent the kibble back for Edmund.

Josette stood waiting for Edmund. She felt warm and opened her winter jacket. Edmund came down the mine shaft and saw Josette waiting with an open jacket. He expected it to be colder in the mine than on the surface, but it was *warmer* at the bottom.

"The temperature down here always stays about 45 degrees," said John Hayes. "Warm in winter, cool in summer."

Josette looked around. The underground room they had reached was as big as their house. "Is this where the miners dig out copper?" she asked.

"Yes, it is," said John Hayes. "Just look at the walls."

Josette and Edmund examined the walls while John Hayes shone his lantern on them. "It looks like there are veins of copper still in the walls," said Edmund.

"But not enough copper for us to spend the time and money to dig it out," explained John Hayes.

Josette noticed an opening in the wall but couldn't see very far into it. "Is that another room?"

"Yes," said John Hayes. "That's an exploratory passage. We abandoned that one when we found only small amounts of copper there." He pointed to some tools left lying on the ground. "One man holds the drill while two others hit it with a sledgehammer. The sledgehammer weighs about twenty pounds. That's how we extract the copper."

"Sounds like hard work," observed Edmund.

Their host nodded. "Sometimes the men have to lie on their backs all day. Sometimes they're on their knees. And sometimes they stand up all day," said John Hayes.

"What's this?" Josette asked, spotting what looked like shiny copper tools.

"I saved those for you to see. We found them while we were drilling." He picked up and handed Josette three small objects. "These are Indian spearheads beaten out of copper," he said.

"Did Indians mine copper?" Edmund asked.

"It appears they did," said John Hayes. "In some places we found traces of early hammer marks on the rocks."

"How long ago?" Josette said.

"We don't know," John Hayes answered. "Maybe thousands of years ago. They had only hammers and cold water and fire to extract pure copper. I'm going to send these copper spearheads to Washington to the Smithsonian, along with some samples of pure native copper for the museum. Experts there will be able to date them."

"What's that noise?" Josette asked suddenly. "It sounds like somebody's running underneath us. Are there miners still down below?"

"Those are rats," said John Hayes, "but don't be alarmed. It's a healthy sign. When rats leave, it means trouble! If they don't have enough air to breathe, neither do we."

Josette hoped that she would not see a rat, even though they were a sign of healthy air.

"How do you get the ore out of the mine?" asked Edmund.

"We use a large bucket, called a kibble, and raise it by ropes. Then we crush the ore on the surface, or, if there are big lumps of copper, we put them in barrels. All the copper is hauled away to the dock by horses."

"Is this the end of our visit?" Josette asked. There didn't seem to be anything more to see, and she thought she heard water gurgling beneath her feet.

"There won't be many more visits to this mine," John Hayes remarked. "My men are picking up the equipment, and then we're closing the mine for good. We'll fill in the shaft before we leave so no one falls in."

Josette grabbed her candle from the timber that had been holding it and climbed back into the kibble to go back to the surface. As she got further up, she noticed light gradually coming into the opening. By the time she reached the surface, the sunlight was so brilliant on the snow that she had to shade her eyes. She quickly tied up her jacket again. The air was cold! When John Hayes reached the top, she said to him, "Now I've got something to write about in our newspaper. Private Wilks and I are going to publish the *Fort Wilkins Agate*, and this will make an interesting story."

Josette and Edmund thanked John Hayes for the trip down in the mine. "Will we see you again?" Edmund asked.

"I hope so," said John Hayes, "but I'm having a new house built at the Cliff Mine so I won't have to travel from there back to Copper Harbor every day. If that mine is as good as it looks, I'm going to be up there for quite a while. Maybe a couple of years."

"But if you come to Copper Harbor, will you visit us?" Josette asked.

"You can count on it," said John Hayes.

His men began to arrive, and he joined them to gather tools and to close the mine.

On her way back home, Josette stopped to watch soldiers on the lake. Since December the water had been freezing gradually, a little bit every day and even more every night. Now ice completely covered the lake. It was frozen solid, and there was no chance of anyone falling through into frigid water.

Josette saw soldiers out on the lake cutting ice and chopping it into blocks while others lifted the cut blocks up into a wagon, its floor covered with sawdust. Soldiers on the wagon spread sawdust over the blocks of ice and stacked them in layers. When the wagon was full, the horses would pull it to the icehouse, where soldiers there would unload the blocks of ice for storage. The sawdust would insulate the ice and keep it frozen for months. It would last into summer, and when warm weather came, the cooks would use it to keep meat and milk fresh.

Josette was tempted to run and slide on the ice, but she knew Edith was waiting for her. Besides, her feet were getting cold.

"I'm home," she called out as she opened the door to their house.

"I've been waiting for you," said Edith. "You stayed down in the mine a long time."

"I wouldn't want to be a miner," said Josette, shivering.

"I should think not!" said Edith. "I don't know any girl miners. That's work for boys and men."

"That's not why," said Josette. "I'd be afraid of rats."

"There are worse things than rats," said Edith. "Like sickness. Private Wilks stopped by to tell me that four soldiers have come down with chills and sweats, and now Private Jones isn't feeling very good, either."

"Private Jones!" exclaimed Josette with concern.

"Yes, I know he's one of your favorites. I'll leave you here to take care of Miles while I go to the hospital to see if I can help."

Edith was gone for what seemed a very long time, and when she came back she looked worried.

"The soldiers are coughing and having trouble breathing," she told Josette. "Private Jones isn't doing well at all."

"May I go to see him?" Josette asked.

"No," said Edith. "We don't want you getting sick. I'm going to make some beef broth and take it over to the hospital."

While Edith was making the broth, Josette started working on her newspaper. She decided there should be an article on sickness at the fort in January 1845. She would have to interview Dr. Isaacs and the soldiers, too, when they were better.

The pot of beef broth was ready, and Edith was just beginning to wonder how to carry it to the hospital when Edmund arrived home for dinner. "I'll carry that pot over," he offered, "but the men will want to see you. You may even have to feed some of them. I stopped in at the hospital on my way home, and Dr. Isaacs says they're very sick."

After Edith and Edmund left, Josette thought more and more about Private Jones. She hoped he wasn't going to die.

CHAPTER TWENTY-TWO

dog

Edith returned from the hospital with an empty pot. That was a good sign. "At least I got some nourishing liquid into them," she said, "but Private Jones had trouble swallowing."

"Will he be all right?" Josette worried.

"I think he's feeling a little better," said Edith. "After I fed him the broth, he tried to sing, but his voice was hoarse."

"Is Edmund still at the hospital?"

"No. Captain Clary sent a soldier over to the hospital to get Edmund. Captain Clary wanted to see him immediately," said Edith.

Just then Edmund walked in the door, saying, "I've got interesting news!"

"About Maria?" Josette asked hopefully.

"No," said Edmund, "about us. Captain Clary just received a letter from the Secretary of War asking if Captain Clary thought Fort Wilkins needed to stay open, since no trouble has occurred with Indians."

Edith gasped. "Does that mean that we can go back to Virginia?"

"We're not jumping to any conclusions yet," said

Edmund, "but Captain Clary is going to recommend to the Secretary of War that we close the fort sometime this spring or summer, unless trouble with the Indians develops."

"If we leave the fort, I'll never see Maria again!" cried Josette.

"Nothing is certain yet," said Edmund, "but there are rumblings on the Mexican border. Our two Companies may be called up to fight a Mexican-American War."

"Would we go along with you if that happened?" Edith asked.

"If there's war along the Mexican border, I'll have to go alone. You and Josette and Miles would have to stay behind in Virginia."

"Will I ever see Maria again?" Josette asked. She didn't like the idea of moving back to Virginia now that she had the best friend in the world up here in the North.

"If we do leave," said Edmund, "I'll try to get to L'Anse so you can see Maria before we go."

She appreciated Edmund's offer, but Josette thought of all kinds of obstacles. "How can we get to L'Anse by canoe without Maria's father? We'd drown!"

Edmund could tell Josette was worried. "There are other ways to get to L'Anse if we go before spring, while there's still snow. There's the possibility of getting a dog team. Or going on snowshoes. I'll try to think of something," he promised. "But just remember, nothing is certain yet. We may still be here for another winter. And this winter isn't half over yet."

Josette thought of something else. "Is the mailman still here?"

"Yes," said Edmund, "he's eating dinner with the

soldiers. He wants to give his dog team a rest, then he'll be leaving in an hour or so."

"Can I give him a letter for Maria?" Josette asked. "I'll ask her to come to the fort one more time if she can before we leave. Her father could bring her on snowshoes."

"Ask her mother to come, too," said Edith.

Edmund didn't want Josette to be disappointed. "If you write her now, I'll go with you to find the mailman so we can make sure Maria gets your letter in L'Anse."

Josette sat down to write to her friend. After she explained to Maria that the fort might be closing in spring or summer, she asked Maria and her mother and father to come to the fort, if they could, for hello and goodbye. She asked Maria to come soon, and she asked Maria to ask her father if he would show Private Wilks how to build a birchbark canoe, just in case they stayed at Fort Wilkins, after all. Then she and Edmund went to the mess hall and handed the letter over to the mailman.

He was just getting ready to leave. "I'm heading for Eagle Harbor and Eagle River," he said, "where I'll stay overnight. Then I'll leave for L'Anse. It may take at least two days to get there, depending on the weather. But I'll deliver your letter personally to Maria."

As Josette and Edmund were leaving the mess hall, Private Wilks called out to Josette. "How about working on the newspaper this afternoon? Rumors are flying that we may be leaving Fort Wilkins for Mexico, and we want to get at least one edition out."

"I have a lot of material," said Josette. "I'll get it and be right back."

Edmund was glad to see that Josette had cheered up. He hoped Maria could come one more time before they left. He knew how hard it would be for Josette never to see Maria again.

The next few days Josette and Private Wilks worked hard on the newspaper. One of Josette's stories was about the soldiers in the hospital. All the sick men were feeling better, Edith told her, and Dr. Isaacs said that in a few days they could go back to the barracks. They were well enough for Josette to interview them. Private Jones's voice was returning, and he and Josette sang duets, including one of his favorites, "Drink to me only with thine eyes, and I will pledge with mine."

Josette and Private Wilks were surprised at how many good writers there were at the fort. One soldier had written about Christmas Eve, another about Christmas Day. Edith had written about the birth of Miles and how Maria's mother, an Ojibwe woman, had delivered him. Edith also wrote about the baptism of Miles by Father Baraga. One of the soldiers told the story of how Father Baraga had come from Slovenia to minister to Indians in the Northern Peninsula of Michigan, miles from his homeland. Josette and Private Wilks wrote the story of the sinking of the *John Jacob Astor*, and Edmund wrote the story of John Hayes and the mine that John Hayes had just outside the fort.

But all Josette's work with Private Wilks on the newspaper was tinged with sadness. The thought of returning to Virginia was a dark cloud hanging over her happiness. She realized how much she would miss the fort, her good friends like Private Wilks and Private Hawkins and Private Jones, and most of all, her best friend in the world, Maria, even though Maria now lived miles away in L'Anse.

She would miss the snow, so white and pure it glistened like stars and the feel of snowshoes gliding over fresh snow. She would miss the smell of the fire in the fireplace and in the stove. She would miss the warm glow in a house that could not be duplicated anywhere and the sound of water swooshing against the shore.

Soon she would have to say goodbye to it all. It seemed only a short time since she had said hello.

CHAPTER TWENTY-THREE

stars

January disappeared in snow. Snow fell every day and every night, and each day blended into the next. Each night was brilliant with stars. The displays in the sky attracted many soldiers out at night. Looking at the vast expanse took away their feeling of being enclosed in a small world that offered no escape.

Everybody wondered if the snow would ever stop. Josette hoped her letter had gotten to Maria in L'Anse. Every day she looked for the mailman, but he never came to the fort. No mailman could get through the deep drifts of January, and the fort didn't get mail for over a month.

Captain Clary and Edmund tried to keep the soldiers' morale high so they wouldn't get the feeling they were winter's prisoners. Like Josette, every soldier waited for news from the outside world, but none came. Josette tried to cheer them up, and they tried to cheer her up. Since no news came from the outside, the only thing they could do was make their own news. Josette and Private Wilks worked hard on the newspaper, knowing how much the soldiers would appreciate reading about their life in the north. By the middle of February the edition was finished.

Private Wilks posted a note in the mess hall asking for volunteers to print copies of the paper, and twenty soldiers volunteered. If these soldiers hand-printed five copies each, they would have enough to distribute a copy to each soldier in the two companies. The nights when the twenty-two workers sat together in the mess hall printing the newspaper were times of good fellowship.

There was one short notice on the back page that the soldiers huddled over with great interest. They didn't talk about it out loud because they didn't want to get their hopes up and because they didn't want to give away the news before their fellow soldiers could read it in print.

When all the copies of the paper were printed, Edmund asked the cooks to prepare a special dinner, and after dinner the soldiers distributed the paper. As soon as a soldier received a copy, he began reading. "Read the last page," one soldier whispered, and the whisper spread through the room. Soon every soldier was reading the last page first.

The article was titled "RUMORS OF CLOSING." The brief note under the headline stated that the soldiers of Companies A and B might be called up to fight in a Mexican-American War that was brewing on the border between the two countries. The companies might be moved as early as May, as soon as the waters of Lake Superior were open to shipping. Each soldier smiled when he read that article.

The only person not happy about leaving Fort Wilkins was Josette. She had been planning a summer with Maria when Maria's family was back in the wigwam. If only she could *talk* to Maria!

At about 3:30 in the afternoon on a Thursday in the first week of March, just as the sky was beginning to get dark, the mailman pulled into the fort on a dogsled. Josette, out on her snowshoes, was the first to see him. She snowshoed over to the entrance of the fort and waved at him and shouted "Hello!"

"Hello!" he called back. "I've got a letter for you from Maria."

Josette snowshoed alongside the dogsled to the mess hall. "Mail!" she shouted happily.

Soldiers streamed out of their quarters, stopping whatever they had been doing. When everyone was assembled in the mess hall, the mailman began to call out names. The first name he called out was "Josette!" The soldiers all applauded.

Josette went home to read her letter aloud to Edith. Maria wrote that she liked living in L'Anse and was working hard in school but that she missed Josette. Then came the news Josette had been hoping for. Maria wrote that she and her mother and father would be coming to Fort Wilkins at the end of the Crow Moon.

"She's coming at the end of March," Josette said happily.

"She can stay here with us," said Edith. "Her parents could stay with us, too, but I expect they will want to stay in their wigwam."

"I'll write a letter back inviting them," said Josette. "The mailman is staying overnight, so I can give him the letter after dinner."

When Edmund got home, he had an official-looking letter in his hand. "Guess what?" he said.

"Are we leaving the fort?" Edith asked.

"Yes," said Edmund. "We'll leave in shifts. Some will leave in May, as soon as the ice jams break up on

Lake Superior and a ship can get through, and by August all the men of both companies will be gone."

"When are *we* leaving?" Josette asked.

"With the first shift" came Edmund's answer. "Things look more and more like a war with Mexico, and I'll be a part of it."

"That's good news and bad news," said Edith. She was happy to be going back to Virginia but not happy about Edmund going to fight Mexico.

"That's the kind of news a soldier gets," said Edmund. "We're trained to defend our country. The soldiers have been restless up here, not doing any fighting."

"I could do without fighting," said Edith, "but I know that's why you went to West Point. And it will be wonderful to see our families in Virginia. They've never seen Miles! But I must say I've grown to like it up here."

The next weeks were long for Josette, even though snow no longer drifted into the fort and the wind no longer howled around the corners of buildings. Every day she snowshoed to the fort entrance and looked for other snowshoe tracks, but all she ever saw were the tracks of rabbits and deer and moose and wolves, along with other animal tracks she could not identify.

One afternoon, just after dinner, she caught sight of something bright red in the distance. She knew it was too early for sunset, though the sun did set in a bright red ball each afternoon. She wondered if it was a cardinal with bright red wings, but she didn't hear a cardinal song.

The red kept coming closer. And closer.

Suddenly she heard a shout, "Josette! Josette!"

"Maria!" Josette called back. "Maria, you've come!"

196

Three figures snowshoed into view. It was Maria and her mother and father. Once again, Maria had kept her promise.

Josette met them outside the entrance to the fort. Maria was wearing the red scarf that Josette had knitted for her for Christmas. Together they made their way to the house.

Edith heard them coming and held the door open. "Come in and get warm," she said. "You can take your snowshoes off in here near the fire."

Josette and Maria couldn't stop talking. Maria's mother went directly to the cradle to see Miles. Maria's father said he would go to the headquarters and talk to Lieutenant Elliott and Private Wilks.

"Will you stay at the fort and show Private Wilks how to build a canoe?" Josette asked Maria's father.

"I would like to show him how to build a canoe," he answered, "but it is too early. First we need to get birchbark, but we must wait for the Planting Moon when the sap runs in the birch trees. Then the birchbark pops off the tree when we cut it. Then we go to the marshes to dig roots of tamarack, balsam and spruce trees. We strip the roots and make them into a strong binding. Now the ground is frozen. We must have patience and wait for the sun to warm the earth again."

"Planting moon is May," said Josette. "That's too late. That's when we're leaving."

"Why are you leaving?" Maria asked.

"Because there's going to be a war between the United States and Mexico," said Josette, "and Edmund has to fight in it."

"Then I won't see you again!" said Maria.

Josette and Maria looked ready to cry. Edith said,

"Now is the time to enjoy each other. Let's not talk about leaving."

Maria's father left for headquarters, and Edith led Maria's mother to the rocker and invited her to sit down. Then she brought Miles to her. He smiled at Maria's mother while she sang him an Ojibwe lullaby, and he seemed to remember that she had been the first person he saw when he was born.

Josette and Maria sat next to the fire and talked. While they were talking, they heard a sound that made them jump up and run to the door. Could it really be? Wasn't there too much snow yet for him to return? The girls went back to their conversation, but then they saw a shadow fly past the window, and this time the sound was clear. "Hiyah . . . hiyah . . . hiyah . . . yuk-yuckle-yuckle."

When they opened the door, there was Gullie. "I wonder if he can catch any fish," Josette said. "The lake is still frozen solid." She went back inside to get crackers for the bird.

When she returned with the crackers, Gullie was happy to have them, but Maria said, "He'll find food in the brook. I can hear the fresh water running."

CHAPTER TWENTY-FOUR

bear sad heart

Maria stayed with Josette for two nights. Her parents slept in their wigwam but came for dinner both nights. On the second night, everyone lingered at the table for a long time after a dessert of apple pie. Nobody wanted to break up the party. Besides, there were important things to talk about.

Edmund started the serious discussion. He explained that the Army had decided to replace their garrison by Company K, 2nd Infantry in case the Indians decided to attack the miners. The Army was sending these soldiers down to the border between the United States and Mexico, where they expected at least a skirmish and maybe a full-blown war over the border dispute involving Texas and California territories. The two countries would try to settle the question of who owned the land by fighting over it. "It looks ugly," said Edmund. "I suspect there will be a war."

"There must be a better way to settle a border dispute," said Edith. "Can't the two countries talk?"

"We're leaving in May," said Josette, "but I want to stay here."

Maria's father listened carefully to Edmund. Then

he said that he hated war. He said that the Ojibwe had never intended to fight with the miners over the territory. The Ojibwe had sold the land to the United States government, and the United States government had given hunting and fishing rights to the Ojibwe so they could still hunt and fish for food and trap animals for the fur trade.

Josette asked Edmund, "Will I be able to see Maria again before we leave in May?" and Maria asked her father, "Can we come to the dock in Copper Harbor when Josette leaves in May?"

"We will try to find out when the ship comes in and when it will leave," her father said, "but I cannot promise. L'Anse is a long way from Copper Harbor, and we may not hear the news in time."

The rest of that night Josette thought about leaving Maria, and Maria thought about how her life was changing. First she had met Josette, the only white girl she had ever seen, and then she and the white girl had become friends. But now they would have to say goodbye to each other. Maria had been taught not to cry, but it was hard to hold back tears.

Edith sensed the girls' sadness. "Why don't you go out and try to count the stars?" she suggested. "They're especially bright tonight."

Anything was better than going to bed and trying to fall asleep with lumps in their throats. They put on their warm coats, and Maria wound the red scarf around her neck. The air was cold outside, but the sky was magnificent. "Hello," someone called to them. It was Private Wilks. "Are you out stargazing, too?" he asked.

"We're trying not to think about leaving the fort," said Josette.

"Leaving is always hard," said Private Wilks, "but

just think: When you're in Virginia and Maria is in L'Anse, you can still see the same sky and think about each other."

That was a good thought. "Now," said Private Wilks, "let's see how many constellations we can find."

They stood outside for about a half hour without getting too cold, but when Maria's mother and father came out on their snowshoes, Josette and Maria knew it was time for bed. "Sleep well," said Maria's mother, "and dream bright dreams about the stars."

Josette and Maria went back inside feeling more cheerful than when they had gone out. They talked about all the good times they had had together. Then they talked about how sad they felt leaving each other. At last Josette said, "We can write to each other. And maybe someday we will come back here, or you can come to Virginia."

"We can write," said Maria, "and yes, maybe someday you will come back to Fort Wilkins."

They fell asleep with a big 'maybe' hanging over them.

The next morning Maria's mother and father came to say goodbye, and Josette put on her snowshoes and accompanied Maria and her parents to the fort entrance. Josette and Maria hugged, even though it was hard to get their arms around each other with all their heavy winter clothes on, and that made them laugh. Then Maria's mother said, "In Ojibwe we do not say 'goodbye.' We say *giga-waabamin*. That means 'I shall see you.'"

As Maria and her mother and father snowshoed away, with the red scarf billowing over Maria's shoulder, Josette called out, "*giga-waabamin!* See you!"

The day was cold. When Josette got back to the house, a few tears had frozen on her face.

By the middle of May word came to the fort that the *Algonquin* would sail into Copper Harbor soon. The ship that would take them away from Fort Wilkins was on its way. Josette helped Edith with the packing. They had more to pack now than when they had come. Edmund arranged for wagons to pick up Edith's piano and all the crates and barrels to be shipped back to Virginia.

Finally the last day at Fort Wilkins arrived. Two sailors from the ship came one afternoon to say the ship was ready to sail. Edmund said the wagons were ready to be loaded and the soldiers would take as much as they could to the ship before nightfall. Edith and Josette watched the soldiers load the piano onto the wagon, and they thought of how music had lifted the spirits of the soldiers at the fort.

By nightfall, the house was empty except for Josette and Edith and Edmund and Miles. Early the next morning, the soldiers packed the belongings of the first group of men who would be leaving the fort, and by noon all the luggage and all the soldiers were in Copper Harbor waiting to board the ship. Josette, Edith, and Miles came on the last wagon from the fort.

It was time for one last dinner in Copper Harbor. François was expecting them. The dinner reminded them of the day they had first arrived. Where would they taste such good roast duck and pigeon and porcupine and venison? Such good gravy? And whitefish in butter, and potatoes, and corn and bean soup? And for dessert, shortcake with rum for the soldiers and cream for "the lady and the little girl"?

François sat next to Josette after dessert was served. "I am sorry to see you go," he said, "but I must tell you. I go home to France this summer."

"Will you come back?" said Josette.

"I don't know," he said. "Copper Harbor will be deserted. Maybe I come back and I go to the Cliff Mines with John Hayes."

By the time dinner was over, everything had been loaded onto the ship. The Captain was waiting on the deck for the passengers, and when he saw Edith carrying Miles, and Edmund carrying the cradle, he said, "This is a good time to sail. The little one won't be seasick. Winds are just right for sailing, and the sea is calm. Look at that blue sky!"

"Hello, little lady," someone called out to Josette.

"Douglas White!" Josette exclaimed. "My friend!"

"What's that you're carrying?" he asked.

"This is a dreamcatcher," Josette told him. "It keeps Miles from having bad dreams."

"Maybe I could borrow it if we have bad weather," Douglas White said. "It's then that I have bad dreams. I remember when the *John Jacob Astor* sank, and I was floating in the water."

"Will we see the *John Jacob Astor* when we leave the harbor?" Josette asked.

"Yes," said Douglas White. "Captain Stannard couldn't get enough equipment to raise it. The hull is still sticking up in the harbor. And will probably be there for many years, until storms take it away."

Soon the ship was ready to sail. Josette and Edmund and Edith, who held Miles, stood at the railing watching the shore disappear. Josette still hoped to see Maria, but there was no sign of her. Something must have kept her from coming to the dock to say goodbye. There on the dock, however, were Privates Wilks, Hawkins and Jones. They weren't leaving until August. They waved big white handkerchiefs, and Josette waved a white handkerchief back. But she was still looking for a red scarf in the crowd.

The ship began to maneuver slowly out of the harbor. Josette and Edith and Edmund were thankful to be sailing on a calm sea on a clear day in May 1845. Now they were passing the skeleton of the *John Jacob Astor*. The Captain avoided shoals and rocks, and as the ship moved farther and farther from the dock, Josette kept waving her white handkerchief.

Finally the ship turned east and sailed out into Lake Superior. Douglas White was looking west when he glimpsed a small craft gaining on them. He said to Josette, "Look over there. That looks like a canoe paddling fast, like it's trying to catch up with us."

Josette turned to look. Somebody in the canoe was waving a red scarf.

"It's Maria!" Josette shouted. "Maria!" she called out to the canoe.

Before the ship had gained too much speed, the canoe pulled up even with it.

"Goodbye, Maria," Josette called, waving her white handkerchief. "Goodbye!"

Now Maria's canoe pulled still closer. The girls could see each other clearly. "See you!" Maria shouted.

Then the ship moved faster, the canoe turned back, and the last thing Josette saw was Maria's red scarf still waving.

"I think I'll take Miles to our cabin for a nap," said Edith.

"I'll bring the cradle down below," said Edmund.

"Would you like to stay on the deck for a while?" Edith asked Josette. She knew that Josette was feeling lonely and that looking out at the disappearing canoe might help.

"I'll take care of her," said Douglas White.

After Edith and Edmund left, Josette said to Douglas White, "There are a lot of gulls following the ship. I wonder what's happening to Gullie. I didn't even think about him when we left."

"Who's that sitting on the railing over there?" Douglas White said, pointing.

"Do you think that's Gullie?" Josette asked.

"Offer him a cracker," suggested Douglas White, handing her a few.

Josette waved a cracker at the gull. It was a beautiful gull with white and gray feathers and a golden beak with a red dot on it.

The gull came to Josette and ate from her hand.

Then he flew back to the railing of the ship and sang a song that she had first heard when she had arrived at Copper Harbor almost a year ago. "Hiyah . . . hiyah . . . hiyah . . . yuk-yuckle-yuckle."

SOURCES

Black, Julie. *Dream Catchers: Myths and History*. Buffalo: Firefly Books, 1999.

Bushnell, G. H. S. *The First Americans*. New York: McGraw Hill, 1968.

Clarke, Don H. *Copper Mines of Keweenaw, No. 1*. Washington: The United States Mineral Agency, 1973.

Danziger, Edmund Jefferson, Jr. *The Chippewas of Lake Superior*. Norman: University of Oklahoma Press, 1979.

Fadner, Lawrence Trever. *Fort Wilkins 1844 and the U. S. Mineral Land Agency 1843*. New York: Vantage, 1966.

Friggens, Thomas G. *Peas Upon a Trencher: A Study of Diet at Fort Wilkins*. Copper Harbor: Fort Wilkins Natural History Association, 1985.

Francis, George. *Legends of the Land of Lakes*. Chicago: G. F. Thomas, 1884.

Jamison, James K. *By Cross and Anchor: The Story of Frederic Baraga on Lake Superior*. Paterson: St. Anthony Guild Press, 1946.

Kah-Ge-Ga-Gah-Bowh. *The Life, History, and Travels (a young Indian Chief of the Ojebwa Nation)*. Philadelphia: James Harmstead, 1847.

Lake Superior Journal: *Bela Hubbard's Account of the 1840 Houghton Expedition,* ed. Bernard C. Peters. Marquette: Northern Michigan University Press, 1983.

Mallery, Garrick. *Picture Writing of the American Indians.* New York: Dover Publications, 1972.

Monette, Clarence J. *The History of Copper Harbor Michigan.* Lake Linden: Clarence J. Monette, 1976.

Pitezel, John H. *Lights and Shades of Missionary Life.* Cincinnati: Western Book Concern, 1861.

St. John, John R. *Lake Superior Country.* New York: William H. Graham, 1846.

Vecsey, Christopher. *Traditional Ojibwa Religion and Its Historical Changes.* Philadelphia: American Philosophical Society, 1983.

Vizenor, Gerald. *The People Named the Chippewa.* Mineapolis: University of Minnesota Press, 1984.

Swallow	Talk	Talk Together
Teepee	Thunder bird	Tree
Same Tribe	Tracks	Trade
Treaty	Tomahawk	Top Man

Three Years	Wading Birds	Walked-passed
War Bonnet	Raising War Party	War
Water Carrier	Calling for Rain	Weather Clear
Weather Stormy	Whirlwind	Horse (white man's)

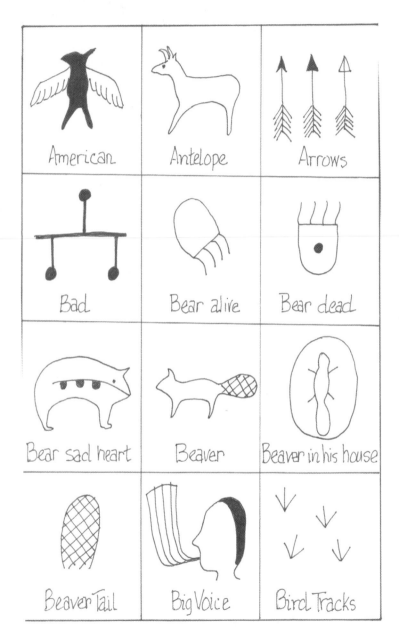

American	Antelope	Arrows
Bad	Bear alive	Bear dead
Bear sad heart	Beaver	Beaver in his house
Beaver Tail	Big Voice	Bird Tracks

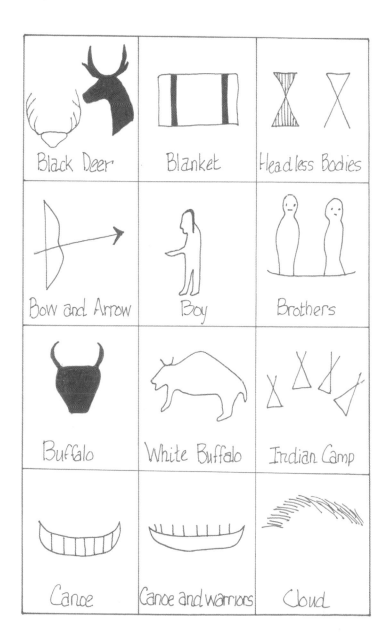

Black Deer	Blanket	Headless Bodies
Bow and Arrow	Boy	Brothers
Buffalo	White Buffalo	Indian Camp
Canoe	Canoe and warriors	Cloud

Corn	Dead	Drum and Stick
Drumstick	Earth Lodge	Geese
Grass	Stone Hammer	I did it
Hidden, Obscure	House	I or Me

Inspired	Meteor	Moon (new hung)
Moon (reached half)	Moon (Full)	Mouse
Otter	Prayer	Shining, Bright moon + Sun
Singing	Snow	Strong

215

Rising Sun	Supplication	Talk (intense)
Travois	Old Tree	Turkey
Turtle	Walk	War
Woods		

White Beaver	White Hawk	White Man
Whooping Cough	Wind	Wolf
Woman	Woman	Winter
Cactus	Canyon	Christian

Cold and Snow	Come or Call for	Plenty Corn
Whooping Cough	Big Crow	White Crow
Council	Crane	Deer, Moose
Direction	Discovery	Dog

Duck	Eagle	Eat
Encampment	Evening	Famine
Fear	Fire	Camp Fire
Fish	Peace Flag	Grove Flag

Hear	Hit	Horse
Horse Tracks	Hungry	Fast Horse
Hunt	Island	Knife
Lake	Lariat	Leggings

Plenty Food	Fort	Fox
Froze to Death	Girl	Goods
Goose	Grasp	Gun
White Hawk	Heart	Hard

Prisoners	Jack Rabbit	Rain and Cloudy
Ran	Rattle Snake	Rest
River	River Fight	River Flood
Road	See	Sea

Three nights	Noon	Omaha Indian
Old	Making Peace	Peace Pipe
Pipe	Pipe	Thunder Pipe
Medecinal Plants	Porcupine	Power

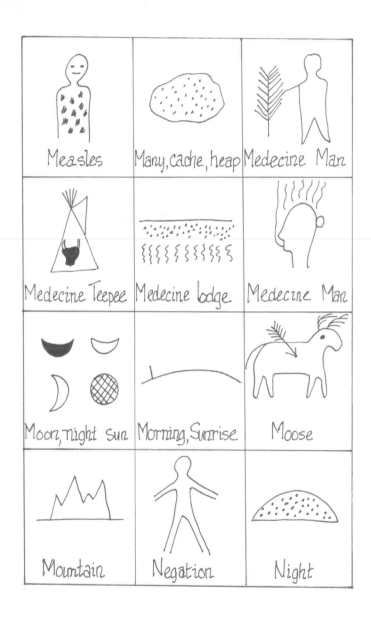

Measles	Many, cache, heap	Medecine Man
Medecine Teepee	Medecine lodge	Medecine Man
Moon, night sun	Morning, Sunrise	Moose
Mountain	Negation	Night

Life	Lightning	Long Hair
Lynx	Man on horse back	Man holding gun
Man	Tall white man	Wise Man
Man Grieves	Man holding bow	Man disabled

Spirits Above	Bad Spirit Medecine	Great Spirit Everywhere
Speaks	Storm and Windy	It struck
Starvation	Stars	Sunrise
Sunset	Sun	Sun

Shell	Mountain Goat	Sick
Sky	Small Pox	Snake
Deep Snow	Deep Snow	Sociability
Soldier	Spotted Face	Spirit

ABOUT THE AUTHOR

Charlotte F. Otten and her family spent many summers in Copper Harbor, Michigan, where she hiked trails to Lake Superior, picked blueberries in a secluded bay, fished for brook trout in Garden Brook, and explored the Keweenaw Peninsula. There she looked at abandoned copper mines, read gravestones in cemeteries, visited Father Baraga's church in Eagle Harbor, Michigan, and spent time at Fort Wilkins. The reconstructed Fort Wilkins is open to visitors—and she visited it often.

Engaged in the study of the fascinating history of Fort Wilkins and Copper Harbor, she began to think of writing a book on living in the Fort in 1844-1845. She discovered which soldiers had been sent there (some with families), which miners had come from faraway places to dig for copper, which Native Americans lived in the territory, and the remarkable itinerary of the Snowshoe Priest, Father Baraga. From that interest sprang *Home In A Wilderness Fort: Copper Harbor 1844* .

Charlotte F. Otten is the author of *January Rides the Wind*, and is a retired Professor of English at Calvin College in Grand Rapids, Michigan.